CLOAKED LEGENDS
The Patriarch

Sheree Elaine

Copyright © 2024 by Sheree Elaine

Cover art by Sarah Buchanan

All rights reserved.

No portion of this book may be reproduced in any form without written permission from the publisher or author, except as permitted by U.S. copyright law.

PROLOGUE

The Creator paced. His white cloak swung out behind him with each turn. His wooden staff, almost as tall as himself, hit the floor with every other step, matching the rhythm of his restless motion. Images of worlds left desolate - people, plants, and animals destroyed - raced through his mind. A dark haze covering each ruined world in a slow swirl of black dust. The dust was the only indicator of the evil that had come and left such devastation. Anyone seeing the world for the first time would assume it never held life at all. This pattern had to be disrupted. He couldn't stand the heartbreak of another lost world.

The Shadow, whose only purpose was destruction, would feed off of the wickedness of the natural state of man. It was what drew the monster to Earth. The Shadow was a master of deceit, chaos, and vile intent. He thrived off the wickedness of men. He entered a world, ruined every decent thing, and then moved on to another world, always leaving a trail of black dust in his wake. For now, he was trapped. But just as the Creator's powers grew each year, so would the Shadow's. His protectors were this world's best hope.

The Creator stopped pacing to watch the golden globe swirling in the middle of the dimly lit room. The sphere was surrounded by slowly rotating golden rings engraved delicately with Latin script. This globe encompassed the time of this earth. It stood as a sentinel, a reminder of the reason for time. That not all things happen at once and that the end of one's time gives life meaning. The circular room had no wall space, only half empty shelves from floor to ceiling. The bookshelves were interrupted only by the doorways that connected to different parts of this world and the one doorway leading into the council room.

He paused before entering the council room, looking at the top shelf to the left of the door. Here was his collection of scrolls and books from the beginning of the creation of this world. Their faded spines and dusty parchment held precious knowledge of worlds that came before, prophecies of the future of this world, words about the Creator himself, and more. His heart wanted to share all knowledge with his protectors, but his head knew the implications of such knowledge. The more you know, the more you are accountable for. He raised his hand and a thick black metal band crossed the middle of the top shelf. He gently touched the band and a soft golden glow spread across the top shelf, completing the seal. Things would be revealed in due time.

He entered the council room and observed the five cloaked figures resting on low tables lined up before him. Studying their faces and knowing their innocence upon awakening confirmed his decision to seal off the books. Empathy, devotion, remembrance, respect, and leadership where a few of the gifts these protectors could provide.

With a great exhale, the Creator raised his hand and felt power leave him. He leaned on his staff for support. The five figures sat up slowly, looking at each other, then at him. Their countenance was serene, almost tranquil. They each stood from their table at their own pace. Each protector had a cloak draped across their shoulders, the hoods lifted and shielding their face. The Creator raised his hand again, and the tables vanished. The newly born protectors waited expectantly.

"I've brought you about for a purpose," the Creator said into the silence of the room. Each of the cloaked figures stood with rapt attention, their only movement the blink of their eyes adjusting to seeing for the first time. "A creature of darkness has entered this world. Increasing greed and selfishness among the people brought him here. He is called The Shadow, for that is where his deeds lie. He is bound, but he will escape. I've brought you here to protect the people and this earth. Your cloaks will help you blend in through the generations. You will see wars, suffering, and chaos. You will also see light and goodness, sacrifice, and love. Each of you has a divine nature that has been prepared for the protection of this earth – powers that you alone wield." He picked up the first of the five staves leaning on the wall behind him and offered it to the figure cloaked in red.

"Nick." Recognition flickered in the cloaked man's blue eyes. He knew his name. "Take this." Nick reached out from beneath his cloak and wrapped his hand around the staff. He held firmly to the staff as a red glow began carving its way up the wood. The carving wrapped upward in swirls and delicate lines. As the light reached his hand, a warmth came through the carved wood and filled Nick's soul. All signs of being recently awoken were gone. He stood firm on his feet, filled with confidence in the presence of his Creator. But there was more. He felt things beyond himself, beyond the walls of this room. At first the feelings were warm, comforting, strengthening. His chest expanded, and he felt his heart swell. Love, excitement, trust, and joy each took their turn running through him. A tear escaped his eye, rolling down his cheek, into his white beard as each emotion consumed him. He gazed lovingly at the Creator, grateful for this gift. Then something much darker infiltrated his thoughts. With a twist in his stomach, he felt pain, suffering, and grief. His hand went to his chest. He felt as if a band wrapped around his heart – betrayal, heartbreak, loss. His eyes shut against the pain, his legs shook, and a tension crept from his shoulders, to the back of his neck, to his head. Nick clung to his staff, the only thing keeping him on his feet. Just when he felt as though the darkness would consume him, he felt a hand on his shoulder. The gentle pressure was a lifeline, pulling him out of the darkness and helping him find the balance. As the memory of the light returned and the darkness retreated, his legs received their strength. He looked up into the sympathetic eyes of the Creator. They didn't need any words. Nick could see the understanding in his eyes.

"Your gift will lift and inspire. Remember the balance. You must maintain a balance and cling to the good in order to keep the darkness at bay. These protectors will look up to you. Love them, guide them, council with them. This world needs all of you." Nick nodded his acknowledgement. "They will look to you to lead." The Creator looked deeply at him, infusing him with a feeling of love and strength before moving on to the next cloaked figure. Nick watched, processing all the emotions he could feel. He tried to sift through and identify where the feelings were coming from, which were his and which came from beyond these walls. That is when he realized – he couldn't feel anything from inside the room, only himself. The Creator had moved on from the man in the blue cloak next to him and was talking to the woman in the ivory cloak. He focused his own feelings and set them aside, making room to reach out to the others in the room, but still felt nothing. His gift was not for them.

Nick watched the Creator talk to each individual, handing each their staff. Every staff's designs glowed in a color that matched its owner's cloak as they placed their hand on it for the first time. Nick couldn't hear the words, but he saw the others' reactions as they received their own name, staff, and gift. The Creator took extra time with the last protector, cloaked in gold. When he finished speaking with her, he stood before them once more.

"I cannot stay. Help one another as you come to know your powers. Lean on each other's strengths and use them to help the people. The time will come when the Shadow is released. Do not fear. You have everything you need amongst yourselves." The Creator looked to each protector, his breathing steady and sure. "Stay close to me." And with those parting words, the Creator left the five protectors. They glanced curiously at one another. No one spoke. Nick knew he would be the first to speak. Somehow, he knew it was part of his purpose in the Creator's plan. He lifted his hand to lower the hood of his cloak, stepped forward and turned to the others. Two men, two women. Each with a different colored cloak and matching staff. Each with an individual purpose to serve the people of the earth. They had much to learn about each other and this world.

"I'm Nick."

CHAPTER 1
(Centuries Later)

The copper railing was cool under Nick's hands. He gripped it tightly, the muscles in his forearms flexed. He maintained a perfect posture, though his shoulders appeared tense and his eyes were hooded as they gazed without seeing. His eyes held wisdom, knowledge gained from centuries on this earth, but his body remained unchanged from the day of his creation. He lifted a hand from the railing to run a hand through his white hair, moving the hood of his cloak to lie atop his back. His hair conflicted with the age he'd been created. Most thirty-five-year-old men were beginning to see a gray hair or two, but not many had a head full of thick, snow-white hair. He shifted his weight, causing his leg to brush against the large black duffle bag that lay at his feet.

His deep blue eyes followed the movement of the golden globe in the middle of the room as it slowly rotated and flickered. Five rings circled the sphere, like rings around a planet. Nick always appreciated the beauty of the Time Room, but it also represented the weight of his calling on this earth. Nick's eyes followed a ring on a complete rotation around the sphere, and then he shifted his focus to a different ring. He reflected on the time he had been on the earth and all the time he still had. He had witnessed times of war, moments of peace, the rise and fall of dictatorships and monarchies, the shift in power across the globe. There had been so much need and want, but also much strength and resilience.

To Nick, the rings represented the five generations that were currently on the earth. Rarely were six generations present, and if they were, the oldest was ancient and the youngest very new. Nick smiled at the thought, then his face returned to its somber stare. Each generation that he'd seen come and go had brought with it new ideas and creations. However, since the turn of the century, it felt as if more was being lost than gained.

"I thought you might be here!" a voice called from a door opposite his position. Nick lunged for his staff that he'd left leaning against the wall behind him. As his hand closed on the wooden staff, a warmth filled his hand and its carved lines lit with a brilliant red glow before returning to its solid oak color. The feeling was so familiar, he barely noticed. He swung the staff around him and it landed right on the chest of the intruder, stopping him from coming closer. Before he could register the man's blonde hair and gray eyes, a familiar jovial laugh reached his ears.

"Jack. You startled me," Nick grumbled.

"I would've thought you'd see me coming." Jack said, knocking Nick's staff off his chest with his own staff made from the same wood but with its own original design. Nick knew Jack's staff would glow blue when he picked it up.

"If you sing that song again..." Nick's threat died on his lips as Jack hummed the lyrics to a famous Christmas song. Nick stepped back, reigning in his annoyance, and trying not to glare too harshly at his friend. He gave Jack a gentle shove with the end of his staff and returned it to the wall behind him.

"You're early," Nick said. He leaned his back against the railing, facing Jack, arms crossed. Jack stared at him for a moment before moving to stand next to him, mimicking his position. It may be Nick's imagination, but despite Jack's playful nature, he always seemed to bring a physical coolness with him.

"Right to the chase, then? No, how are you? What have you been up to in the last decade or so?"

"I see you in council every year."

"Right, but it's been a year since the last and our paths haven't crossed. Those meetings, thanks to you, are always short and to the point. Then we head our separate ways."

"We're busy and there isn't much new to report from one year to the next."

"Yes, but when was the last time we had a genuine conversation?" Jack gave Nick's arm a playful nudge.

"You came to talk?" Nick's eyebrows were low, accentuating the fine lines around his eyes.

"Honestly, I came for this." Jack turned around and waved his hand toward the golden sphere. "Seeing you and getting to have this lovely conversation is just a bonus," Jack said cheekily. Nick turned to face the globe as well. He could understand the draw to the Time Room. The centuries of scrolls and books collected and piled into the bookshelves gave the room a reverent feeling. Nick felt a sense of wonder every time he returned to the place where they had once been created. This room, outside the dimension of the rest of the world, was a place they could retreat to, a place to feel closer to the Creator, and meet for council each year. It was a wise, much appreciated gift.

"It's peaceful and a great chance to center my thoughts before council," Jack continued, rolling onto the balls of his feet and back down again. Nick wondered if perhaps he wasn't the one Jack had hoped to run into. As their historian, Allie was the one in and out of this room most often. Nick pushed aside that thought as a strange darkness entered his mind. A feeling of loss and despair coupled with a physical hunger and overwhelming weariness. He'd learned early in his time on the Earth to act on these promptings from the Creator. An inconvenience, large or small, is nothing compared to the shame of failure caused by not heeding the Creator's call.

When the Creator left, Nick entered an unknown world with very little preparation. He stumbled along with the others, but through practice and patience he'd learned to decipher the tug in his heart leading him to do the Creator's will. Sometimes it was soft, almost like a suggestion. Other times, like now, it felt almost like a physical force pulling him toward his next assignment. The more he listened, the easier it was to tell the Creator's will from his own.

"You want to talk?" Nick said, meeting Jack's gaze. "Walk with me. I'm needed in New York."

"Now?" Jack asked, looking toward the council room and back at Nick.

"Yes, now. We'll be back in time for council. Come." Nick picked up his staff and walked toward the door that had the words New York City Library carved into the wood above it. An analog clock hung above the door frame with the local time. Allie's desire and talent for organization had often come in handy and adding these signs above the door was one of Nick's favorite improvements that she'd made to the Time Room. It was quite disorienting to think you were walking into the New York Library, only to come out in the Tianjin Binhai Library in China.

A few hundred years ago, Kaida had orchestrated the effort to have libraries built at the entrances to the Time Room. Some had taken longer than others, but the efforts had been worth it. As each destination's country developed, they engaged in local politics and networked with leaders to ensure the libraries were built in the right place. Kaida had a knack for politics. Her ability to speak and understand all languages came in handy, but her sharp mind and quick wit won over the people and other political leaders. Nick always believed she could charm the world if given the chance. The libraries had been a group effort - their last – now that Nick thought of it. They made the transition between different parts of the world easier. He placed his hand on the handle of the door, glanced back to make sure Jack was with him, and the two of them walked through.

CHAPTER 2

The pull intensified as Nick entered the New York City Library. He rushed to the back row of books, with Jack trailing behind. Nick glanced around the end of the shelf to see the octogenarian librarian checking out books for a teenage patron. Nick couldn't help smiling as the two discussed a book the teenager was borrowing. The enthusiasm they shared for the same author created an instant connection between the two. Books had that kind of power. Nick gestured for Jack to follow quickly, and they exited the library without notice.

The December air chilled Nick's face, and he lifted his hood to shield his face from the frigid wind. His cloak kept the rest of him warm. He knew from past experience entering New York through this library that they were on 53rd street. They headed west, the hood of his cloak shielding his eyes against the setting sun. People heading home from work or heading out for the night congested the sidewalks. The cars, tour buses, and taxis in the streets were bumper to bumper as they all attempted to arrive first. The noise of the streets and the unique smell of New York seemed distant to Nick as he followed the intense feeling of despair coming from the one that had the Creator tugging at his heart. It led his feet swiftly through the crowds, his shoulder jostling people as they walked past. Each person he walked past or touched gave him a surge of emotion. Crowds like this often became overwhelming and Nick was missing the solitude of the Time Room. He felt the urge to follow these particular feelings, and that's exactly what he'd do. They turned on 10th and then again on 52nd. There was a food cart parked on the corner. He stepped up to the window and saw a middle-aged man sitting on a tall stool, looking at his phone.

"Are we headed to Jersey?" Jack asked, slightly winded from trying to keep up.

"A bagel with cream cheese please," Nick said, ignoring Jack and pulling some cash from his cloth carrier bag he kept slung across him beneath his cloak. It was a gift he'd received in Mexico many years ago.

"Plain, Asiago or blueberry?" The man's gruff voice asked briskly.

"Blueberry," Nick said, handing the man a ten-dollar bill. "And a water bottle, please. You can keep the change." Nick's heart swelled with gratitude and he recognized it as the emotions of the food vendor. Now he wished he'd paid with a twenty. He turned to Jack as the man prepared the bagel.

"No, not Jersey. We're not far now," he answered. "What *have* you been up to in the last decade or so?" Nick asked before taking the bagel from the vendor. He wrapped the bagel in the napkin and slipped it and the water into his bag. He slowed his steps so Jack could walk alongside him instead of jogging behind him.

"I'm so glad you asked!" Jack said genially. "Let's see, I'm sure you heard about the tsunami in the Aleutian Islands..."

"That was you? I heard there was a magnitude of destruction. People had to leave their homes. People that had been there for generations."

"It wasn't me," Jack said, throwing up his hands defensively, "but I went to help with the cleanup. I tried my best to calm the winds around the waters while I was there. They should have many years before another tsunami hits. They can rebuild and fortify to be better prepared for future storms. You know the ocean is one element that isn't controlled. Ben can encourage and calm the waters, but the entire ocean is too much for anyone other than the Creator himself." There was a moment of silence between them at the gravity of the Creator's power. His power warranted their respect and awe.

A young mom came around a corner toward them, holding hands with a small boy. A Bernese mountain dog's leash was in her other hand and she was being pulled in two different directions. The boy stopped to look at a pile of leaves and the mom let go of his hand. She had to use both hands and all her weight to stop the massive dog from jumping on the two men. Jack took a subtle step behind Nick as the dog jumped and barked. A sudden wind whipped around in front of them, causing the pile of leaves the small child was observing to twirl in a small tornado around the boy. He laughed as the leaves brushed against his cheeks. The dog became distracted by the leaves and the boy's laughter. The young mom regained control of the dog and grabbed her son's hand again. Nick and Jack continued along without incident.

"Come on, Trey." The mom said sternly, turning and tugging on the boy's hand. She glanced suspiciously behind her and Nick felt her uneasiness at their closeness as they passed. His heart was heavy, thinking of how far this world had changed. A mother couldn't even walk down the street without her protectiveness and suspicion flaring around strangers.

"Still not a fan of dogs, I see." Nick said to Jack. "The leaves were a nice touch." He looked toward Jack, one eyebrow raised. The sudden swirl of leaves was a classic Jack move.

"I'll leave the animals to Ben. They really aren't my thing." Jack admitted. "And thank you, the leaves were the least I could do. She had her hands full. She definitely wouldn't have accepted help from two strange men passing through this part of town."

Nick caught his reflection in the store window and paused. In the window he saw himself in a suit and long dark coat, a red scarf around his neck and a matching winter hat. His winter gear was the same shade of red as his cloak. It was a professional, dignified look, especially with his white hair. It made him look older than he was. Well, younger since he had been on earth for centuries, but older than his body, that was around thirty-five. He looked at Jack's reflection and noticed that Jack was similarly dressed, but with a blue scarf and hat that matched his cloak. Nick wondered at Jack's lack of facial hair, thinking his face must be cold.

The Creator was wise in giving them these cloaks. It allowed them to blend in wherever they went. Cloaks had been fashionable in a few places in the world in various times throughout history, like the renaissance and even medieval times, but he could only imagine the looks he'd get walking down any main street in his bright red cloak if it didn't transform his image to fit the era and location.

Jack was looking at the store as well, but not at their reflections. He was looking through the window at the statue of Santa next to a display shelf of toys.

"It must be hard to get away from that guy this time of year," he said, pointing. Nick began walking again and Jack followed, taking a hurried step to fall in line beside him.

"It gets old pretty quick," Nick admitted.

"They got the white beard right. And hey, at least they gave you Mrs. Claus. I'm still the lonesome fellow that brings the winter," Jack said with a laugh. "How is the missus, by the way?" Jack joked, wagging his eyebrows. Nick had grown to expect these kinds of comments from him. Jack found amusement in the legends that people had built around each of them, more than any of the others did.

"Ha. Ha," Nick deadpanned.

"You mean - Ho ho ho, right?" Nick took a few steps forward and began walking backwards, twirling his staff next to him as he walked, no doubt to see Nick's expression at the teasing.

"Okay frosty, let's do this so we can be back in time for council," Nick said.

"I'm not sure what *this* is, but I'm along for the ride, enjoying your sunshiny company," Jack replied. Nick gave a big fake grin that made his nose and eyes crinkle before letting the smile drop and looking around Jack.

"Always so serious," Jack mumbled, turning back around. Normally, Nick's comeback would be on the seriousness of their responsibilities to the people of earth. Sometimes he would say they couldn't all be as carefree as Jack always seemed to be, but he let the topic drop. They had arrived at their destination.

They stood at the end of a dark alley, shadowed even more by the setting of the sun. Two large brick buildings, one a pawnshop and the other an abandoned clothing store, bordered the alley. The corridor appeared empty, but Nick knew better. He could feel a desperate soul close by, the one he'd felt drawn to help. He tightened his grip on his staff and began walking slowly toward a dumpster halfway down the passageway. The mixed odor of trash, urine, and musk from the Hudson River was nauseating. As they came around the dumpster, Nick heard Jack's sharp intake of breath and he steadied himself for this encounter.

CHAPTER 3

Nick watched the filthy, thin blankets rise and fall with the homeless man's deep breathing. This was the soul the Creator had called him to from the Time Room. The despair and hopelessness emanating from him felt suffocating. Nick took a centering breath, found his balance, and squatted down next to the man. He reached a hand into his cloak, opened his bag, and pulled out the bagel with cream cheese.

"Sir," Nick said, gently nudging the man's arm. "Sir," he said more forcefully when the man didn't move. If Nick couldn't sense the man's emotional distress, he would be inclined to think they had arrived too late, and that this soul had returned to the Creator. On Nick's third attempt, the man woke with a start and sat up bleary-eyed, pulling his blankets up to his chin. His mouth was pulled down and surrounded by deep wrinkles and skin that hung from his face. He had a slightly emaciated look, possibly from malnutrition or substance abuse—most likely both. The man's wrinkles were caked with dirt and his jacket hood hung on by a thread. His hair was in a loose ponytail, wayward strands stuck to the dirt on his face. His beard, gray like his hair, was uneven and scraggly.

"I ain't breakin' no law. I have as much right to be here as anyone. I won't move," he ranted angrily with a gruff New York accent. After a pause, the anger in his eyes faded into desperation, and he whispered, "Don't make me move."

"We're not the police, and we're not here to make you move. This is for you," Nick said, holding the bagel toward the man. "What's your name?" The man looked at them suspiciously.

"What do you want?" He asked with a snarl, showcasing one yellowed front tooth, the other missing.

"We're just here to talk," Nick said, looking at Jack, who quickly nodded his agreement.

"What's your name, sir?" Jack asked.

"Name's Calvin. I used to go by Cal." He reluctantly reached for the bagel. Calvin's fingers poked through the ends of his gloves, which weren't much cleaner than the blankets around him. Realizing that the food would not be snatched away from him, he took a giant bite and leaned back against the brick wall. His filthy blankets settled in his lap.

"Nice to meet you Calvin. I'm Nick. This is Jack," Nick said.

"What do you want?" Calvin asked again around a second bite of bagel.

"How long have you been out here? Do you have any family nearby? The weather is getting worse. Do you have any other place to sleep? Indoors perhaps?" Nick asked.

"I don't know, no, and no. I get by." Nick felt the pride and shame battling inside Calvin for dominance.

"There's a shelter just around the corner. Do you ever stay there?" Nick asked. Calvin didn't answer for a long while.

"I get by," he repeated, tugging his blankets higher on him. Nick watched Calvin as he continued to eat his bagel in large bites. The homeless man's calm, stubborn exterior might have fooled some, but Nick could feel the warring emotions inside him. He pulled out the bottle of water, removed the lid, and handed it to Calvin. He lifted it to his mouth and gulped half the water in one breath. The water trickled down one side of his mouth and into his matted beard. Calvin lowered the water and wiped his chin.

"Would you allow us to walk you to the shelter? They have resources for helping those in your situation," Nick asked cautiously.

"You don't know my situation," Calvin barked. Nick made a point of looking around the dark alley before looking back at Calvin.

"Perhaps not, but it seems dire. It's only going to get colder." When the man protested again, Nick raised a hand. "We won't impose where we aren't wanted. It was a pleasure to meet you, Calvin. May I call you Cal?" Nick reached out a hand to shake Calvin's and the man just stared. Slowly, he raised a dirty gloved hand and clasped Nick's. The moment they made contact, Nick felt skeptical, untrusting, and hardened. An invasion of Calvin's tumultuous emotions. He quickly separated the man's emotions from his own and thought of one word. A word to help this man. *Worthy.* He transferred the word to the man, hoping it would take root and grow. He dropped Calvin's hand.

"Let's go, Jack," Nick said, straightening to his full height. They took a few steps and Jack stopped, looking back.

"We can't just leave him," Jack said in a low voice. "He'll freeze. What was the point of walking all the way out here if he's just going to stay?"

"Just keep walking. Trust me," Nick answered, lightly pushing Jack to keep him moving. They had made it to the end of the alley when they heard a voice behind them.

"Stop. Wait." They turned to see Calvin stumbling toward them with a plastic grocery bag in his hand. His blankets draped over his arm. "I... uh..." he looked at the ground instead of their faces. Nick stepped toward him and placed an arm around his shoulders.

"Let's go, Cal." They walked him the six blocks to the shelter. Calvin paused outside the doors, looking side to side as if ready to bolt. A sharp icy wind blew behind them, pushing Calvin toward the door and making the warmth inside that much more appealing. Once inside the door, Calvin turned to look at the two men. His eyes fell on Nick and he felt the surge of gratitude flow between them. Nick smiled and nodded encouragingly, and Calvin let the door close, leaving Nick and Jack standing on the street.

"That was incredible," Jack said as they walked away from the shelter. "Do you think he'll stay? Will they be able to help him? Will he let them help him?"

"I believe he's had a realization of his own worth and that he deserves to heal. Accepting help isn't easy for anyone," Nick said.

"How did you know he was ready for help?" Jack asked. "The wind and weather have their own set of rules. They all have their own personalities in a way, but humans are so much more complex and opinionated."

"The Creator sent me. He was ready," Nick said firmly. "Now tell me more about what's been going on since I saw you last. Quickly, though, council begins soon." Jack jumped into a story about the Amazon jungle as they walked back toward the library.

CHAPTER 4

"Shoot. I forgot about closing time," Nick said, trying the library door. Locked. Nick and Jack glanced at one another and jogged to the back of the library. In the early years of this library, they had found one window helpful in this situation. They'd had to find alternate entrances to most of the libraries since the Creator's assignments weren't always during convenient open hours. Nick slid a garbage can out of the way, the sound echoing in the space between buildings. A mouse ran out from behind the can and disappeared behind a stack of broken-down cardboard boxes leaning against the brick wall. Nick pushed the window halfway in, pulled back, and then pushed it quickly the rest of the way in and it opened with only a small squeak. They clambered through the window, and Jack closed it behind them. They walked quickly and quietly down the back aisle of books and entered the door that appeared as they approached the southeast corner of the library. Nick was grateful that the cameras at this library were focused only on the entrance and check-out desk.

As soon as they entered the Time Room, they heard a soft static of conversation. Kaida, Allie, and Ben were standing together next to the globe, deep in discussion. Kaida's voice was rising when Jack closed the door loudly behind them in his haste. Most likely, they discussed political differences. Ben fought hard for all environmental issues and felt that Kaida didn't do enough.

"There you two are. We were beginning to worry," Ben said, leaving the women to shake hands with Nick and then Jack. The three of them then walked to join Allie and Kaida, who stood silently watching the exchange. Kaida stood with her hands at her side, her back as straight as a soldier at attention. Her golden cloak matched the slowly rotating globe. Allie leaned to one side with her thumbnail in her mouth, no doubt concerned by the contention between Ben and Kaida. Her auburn hair, pulled back in a bun at the nape of her neck, showcased her dangling book earrings.

Jack went to stand next to Allie. She dropped her hand and looked up at Jack with a shy smile. He beamed down at her, his smile always coming easy.

Nick could not feel the emotions of those in this room, and he welcomed the relief. He still felt the emotions of everyone outside of this room, but unless the Creator sent him to a specific soul, it was easy to set it in the background for the sake of council or meditation in the Time Room.

While he may not feel the protectors' emotions, it didn't stop him from instinctively reading their body language. Something he'd learned without trying because of his gift. Jack was always happy but seemed extra light on his feet standing next to Allie. His elbow reached out to brush the top of her arm, and she looked up at him. Her expression and body language held curiosity and shyness, while Jack's was like a man falling. Centuries of friendship seemed to be becoming more between these two. Nick watched the development with fascination. He looked to Ben, who was watching Jack with a raised eyebrow, his eyes flitting over to Allie, then back to Nick. So, Nick hadn't been the only one to notice. Ben turned away from Nick and glanced toward the door to New Zealand.

Ben seemed slightly on edge, but he always was when he was indoors. Ben's gift was with animals and nature. That was where he was most comfortable. Every time they met at council he seemed the most eager to leave. In the few moments of greeting everyone in the circle, Ben glanced thrice more at the door leading to the Auckland, New Zealand library.

Kaida was the last to draw Nick's attention. He had a feeling she preferred it that way. Her pale perfect skin and almond-shaped dark eyes combined with her shoulder length jet black hair made her a natural beauty, but he also knew her incredible intellect. Kaida knew how to speak and understand every language. It was her gift from the Creator. Of all those in this room, Kaida was the most involved in politics. She had a brilliant talent for it and had served in many countries in the background of the political games.

Staff Assistant, lady-in-waiting to future queens, secretary, envoy - she had many titles over the centuries and her golden cloak made it possible, disguising her properly for each role.

"Now that you two are here, can we begin?" Ben asked, tapping his watch and pointing toward the council room. Everyone murmured in agreement.

CHAPTER 5

The council room had five desks arranged in a half circle. Nick was grateful for the advancement in chairs. The wooden chairs they used for centuries were very uncomfortable, even with the goose feather pillows Allie had sewn as cushions. Modern-day black leather, adjustable office chairs were an immense improvement. Each table had a notebook and pen for notes, a glass of water, and a lamp. Allie again, always the organized one.

Nick took the large duffel he'd left in the Time Room and dropped it into the supply closet. He glanced around the room from the closet doorway as everyone settled in. He couldn't help noticing Ben's increasing unease. It seemed like he was trying to hide it, but Nick noticed the subtle flick of his eye away from everyone and the way he was holding, almost too still, like he wanted to fidget but didn't want to appear nervous. He perched on the edge of his seat, resembling one of his forest animal companions ready to flee at the slightest hint of danger.

Jack sat for only a second before jumping up to whisper in Allie's ear, then returned to his desk. She looked annoyed but flattered, her cheeks tinted a light pink. The light pink became a dark red when she noticed Nick watching the exchange. Jack leaned back casually in his chair with his feet propped on his desk, unbothered by Allie's reaction to him and ignorant of Nick's attention. Kaida sat with her feet tucked under her seat. She pulled a hair tie from her wrist and tied her hair back, ready to begin.

Nick moved to his desk as Allie turned on the recorder. With the advancements in technology, she could record and dictate simultaneously. It wasn't for her and her perfect recall, but for the rest of the protectors. It was beneficial to be able to look anything up after the meeting or from any council meeting in the past hundreds of years. Nick stated they are meeting as a council, the time, and date of the meeting. Allie gave him a nod, and he was free to move on.

"It's good to see everyone again. Sorry to be late, we had an urgent matter to attend to in New York. As usual, we'll go around and give our status reports. Be sure to let us know if you're changing locations or if you have any entreaties. Who would like to start?" After a few seconds of silence, Jack dropped his feet off his desk, slapped his hands on his knees and volunteered at the same time as Allie.

"Oh, you can go," Allie said timidly. She was never one to seek the center of attention.

"No, please, ladies first," Jack said regally before putting his feet back up on his desk. Kaida scoffed and tried to cover it with a cough. All eyes turned to her, but she just shook her head and shuffled through some papers on her desk. Allie moved to the front of the room, cleared her throat and began.

"I have twelve volumes of histories to add to the library this year. Three written this last year and nine that I've been working on properly restoring and that are now ready to be returned to the shelves. I have also made improvements to the notice board." Allie pointed to the corkboard against the council room wall, and Nick saw that there was, in fact, a new decorative border and the sections were labeled differently. Allie hung the notice board many years ago when cork boards were first invented. She was always trying to keep everyone organized, and they each did their best to humor her. The board was where the protectors could leave notes to each other or requests for the next council meeting throughout the year.

"There's an envelope for each of you on the board with all the cash and currencies you've requested, and some extra you can draw from throughout the year. Be sure to make a note on the notice board if there is a different currency you need or if you need more of something this year or next year. Our stocks and bonds are doing amazing thanks to Kaida's keen understanding of the market." She smiled at Kaida, who returned the smile with a dip of her head. "Our figurative cash under the mattress is also still plentiful." She inhaled and looked up, trying to think of anything she might have missed. She exhaled and switched gears. "I know I mentioned this at the last council, but I've grown even more concerned in the past year. We've been experiencing a time of semi- peace, would you say?" She looked around, the answers ranging from Jack's shrug to Kaida's response of, "Semi might be putting it lightly."

"I believe we're tilting towards a time of war. New leaders are rising, not good ones, and it just feels similar to the times that we've seen right before other wars. I don't know if it's a cold war type situation or something bigger. The global pandemic a few years back hurt and helped political tensions. I just felt it was worth mentioning again this year."

"How long do you think we have? Where will it take place? Where are tensions the highest? Is there anything any of us can do to help?" Nick rapid fired, drumming his fingers rhythmically on his desk.

"I'm not sure, maybe a few years. It isn't an exact science. Maybe Kaida has more insight?" Allie turned timidly toward Kaida's desk. Nick didn't quite understand their relationship. Allie always seemed nervous around Kaida.

"If a war breaks out, there will be no location. It will be everywhere," Kaida said stoically, tapping her stack of papers vertically against the desktop to straighten them.

"So casual," Ben scoffed. All heads turned to him and Kaida slowly laid the papers on her desk, running a hand across the top page. "Is there a war coming or not? You act as though war is just another bullet point on our business list. War means lives lost, economic and environmental chaos." Bens grit his teeth and glared between Kaida and Allie. "You think because we've seen the wars come and go that it isn't significant, that it doesn't affect us?" Ben pushed back from his chair and stood, looking at Kaida. Jack dropped his feet to the floor, his eyes glancing toward his staff leaning on the wall behind him.

"You throw out an impending war so casually." Ben continued, "Perhaps you should fight directly in this one, as some of us have in the past. Be in the action, watching your comrades fall left and right. Hear the cries of the mothers who've lost sons, see the faces of children burying their fathers…"

"You think I don't know the seriousness?" Kaida stood as her words came out, barely controlled. "This is not a revolutionary war with inaccurate guns and hand to hand combat. Missiles will be launched and bombs will be dropped. Potentially thousands of dead with the touch of a button. I may not have been on the ground, but I've been in medical tents alongside Allie, bodies lined up from wall to wall. I've been in rooms where they've discussed lives lost as a statistic." Kaida spit out the last word in disgust. "I've lost friends, just as you have. Just as we all have. Don't tell me I don't understand war. Don't confuse my calm for apathy." Her eyes flashed dangerously.

"Enough," Nick directed, rising from his seat. He had never witnessed a temper such as this in Ben. He was always so calm and controlled, as steady as the earth, but now he seemed like a volcanic mountain on the verge of eruption. There had been plenty of heated discussions in this room in the past, but this was getting them nowhere.

"Enough," Nick repeated softly. Ben and Kaida slowly lowered themselves back into their seats. "Let's not make assumptions about how others are feeling. We cannot let the tension of the world affect our judgment in this room. We must stay united in our work to help everyone. Kaida is not your enemy, Ben. Let's take a thirty-minute break and then resume."

"No," Ben blurted. "I'm fine. Let's continue. I apologize for my disrespect and lack of control. It won't happen again." An awkward silence filled the space as the tension slowly dissipated.

"Very well. Thank you, Allie," Nick said. Allie looked at her desk, directly between Kaida and Ben, as if it were the last place she wanted to be. She made her way slowly glancing between the two. Ben sat glowering while Kaida stared at her hands clasped on her desk in front of her.

"Kaida, are you ready to present?" Nick asked.

"Of course," Kaida said, standing to take her place at the front. She was a vision of calmness, but Nick didn't miss the twitch in the corner of her eye or the tightness of her mouth.

"Oh, wait," Allie said, standing again. Kaida paused and took the few steps back to her desk. "I have an entreaty for Jack this year." She turned to look at him, leaning to see around Ben's desk, and Jack straightened in his seat, leaning forward. "The farmers in southern Italy have had an excessive amount of rain. The soil has become waterlogged, and their grapes will struggle in the spring if they don't get a reprieve," she said.

"Which affects the economy and individual families' well beings," Jack added, nodding his understanding. "I can visit right after this council and see what I can do before heading to El Salvador."

"Thank you." Allie stood awkwardly. "I'll just..." she slowly sat back down but before her back hit the chair she sprung up again. "Oh, and I'm staying in Rome but after almost fifty years my apartment building is being renovated so I'm temporarily located across the road and down a ways. If you need me, you can find me, or leave a note on the board." She settled into her chair and turned to Nick, who turned to Kaida.

"I'll just go last," she said, gesturing for Nick to take the front of the room. He did and began his report.

"This past year I've spent a lot of time in the States and Canada. My greatest concern right now is for the youth. Suicide rates and reports of depression and anxiety continue to rise. The studies and reports only show so much. I can feel it. A general sense of melancholy settling across the globe. These ailments are affecting the youth at younger and younger ages. The pandemic was a catalyst, and it seems everyone is struggling to bounce back." His words became faster and louder. "Their technology, social media, and news stations add to the depression. They feed everyone a steady stream of exaggerations and lies. Advancements," Nick air quoted, "in technology make it easy for people to isolate themselves. People become so consumed with themselves that they don't even know the needs of their neighbors." Nick paused and looked up, catching himself.

"Forgive me." He looked around, then down again, collecting his thoughts. When he looked up again he saw the looks of sympathy from the other protectors, and it caused a tightness in his chest. They understood, they saw it too, even if they couldn't feel it the same way he did. Nick rolled his shoulders back and stood tall. "I will spend the next little while in Ethiopia. The wars continue to rage along the Ethiopia and Sudan borders. I'm joining a medical team. I will do what I can to help. In fact, my plane leaves later tonight. My entreaty is for Kaida. If there is any political advantage you've gained that can send support for these displaced families, particularly the women and children, they'd be much relieved." He looked and saw Kaida taking notes.

"I'll see what I can do. Everyone is keeping pocketbooks locked tight these days because of inflation, but I'm sure I can pull some strings and call in favors. In fact," Kaida mumbled the last words to herself as she made more notes, a satisfied gleam in her eye, "I have a plan. I'll be in contact."

"Thank you. Who's next? Jack? Ben?" They glanced at each other and Ben gave a sweeping motion with his arm, giving Jack the stage.

CHAPTER 6

"Before I forget, I am not moving locations. I'll be in and out a lot going to various disaster areas as usual, but home base will be the same place near the Switzerland Library." Nick couldn't help but think about how perfect a location that was for his skiing fanatic friend. Jack suddenly turned his back to everyone. Nick leaned back in his chair and folded his arms. He knew what was coming next. Jack raised the hood of his blue cloak and glanced dramatically to the side.

"Weather patterns are harsh. Spontaneous. The dangers increase. The ground shakes, the ocean rages, but what, I ask, is more devastating than the natural disasters?"

"Your dramatics every time we meet for council," Ben muttered and Allie laughed into her hand. Jack swung around, throwing his cloak behind him.

"Nay, good sir! It is the family," Jack exclaimed. His dramatics reminded Nick of the jousting announcers in medieval times.

"What family?" Ben asked, looking unsure if he should encourage Jack. It felt like he was playing right into the act.

"All family. The nuclear family is being seen as old-fashioned and oppressive in many parts of the world. Birth rates are low, while homeless numbers are astronomical." He glanced at Nick, no doubt remembering Calvin. Jack's voice lowered, his dramatics taking a tragic tone.

"The mental health issues mentioned by our valiant leader, Nick, are causing abuse, neglect, and abandonment. I can help control the weather but family..." He trails off, a loneliness in his eyes. "Kids should have the love of parents and grandparents. Mothers shouldn't be so anxious when passing strangers on the street. Single parents worry about how to get food on the table and manage their day-to-day lives single-handedly. There are so many success stories, but so much heartbreak and struggle." Jack clasped a hand to his chest as if physically pained by his own words. He then sprinted toward his desk and, in one giant leap, assisted by a gust of wind, was standing on top of it. This is a bit much even for Jack, Nick thought, spinning his office chair to the right and looking up at his friend.

"The loud voices, the ones that are coming from a place of pain, selfishness, and pride, are affecting the perspective of the youth. They see family, especially children, as inconvenient and unnecessary. Marriage as well. Everyone will suffer as the deterioration of the family continues. We should protect it. Cherish it. I've found an organization that supports family - marriage counseling, support for single mothers, shelters for the abused, crisis centers. I propose a large donation. All in favor?" Jack leapt from the desk and landed back in the center of the room, throwing his cloak to the side dramatically. Jack looked around. Everyone just stared back. "Good, we all agree. I'll make the donation." He said with a confident smile. He bowed as if ending a performance for the Queen of England.

"How were crops this year in the Midwest?" Nick asked hopefully. Jack looked at Ben. They worked together on a lot of their projects - nature and weather. When they worked together harmoniously, they could accomplish a lot of good. Which wasn't always the case. These two men's personalities were as opposite as their physical appearances. Ben, with his black hair, dark skin and dark eyes, was as steady as stone. Jack, with his light skin, blonde hair, and light gray eyes, was a whirlwind, moving from one project to the next with a flurry of passion and excitement. Both were excellent protectors, but they often disagreed on how to handle logistics. Mostly, Jack annoyed Ben to no end, like the little brother Ben likely viewed him as.

"I've said my piece," Jack said. "Do you want to take over?" He motioned toward Ben.

"Yes." Ben cleared his throat, "Uh, yes." He seemed thrown off by the sudden shift in attention. "What was the question?" Ben glanced toward the council room door again. His body leaned toward the door in anxiousness.

"How were crops in the Midwest this year?" Nick repeated as Jack took his seat, sending a not-so-covert wink to Allie. She still looked shell-shocked by Jack's performance.

"They had a very fruitful year," Ben began. "Jack was able to encourage more rain, and I worked with a university on educating people on proper crop and soil care. During the global pandemic, many people had time to start small hobby gardens and took time to learn how to store food against the season. It's been a beautiful thing to come out of such a troubled era. A regrowth of knowledge from the older generation." He nodded toward Allie and she beamed. Jack glowered momentarily up at Ben, then masked it before anyone noticed. "I have little to share this year, all the same from last year. I'm staying in my same location." A collective groan filled the room.

"You're kidding, right?" Jack exploded.

"Uh, no, I like it there." Ben looked around, confused.

"It's so hard to get to. The build and design are hundreds of years old. Have you even updated to modern plumbing?" Kaida asked, bewildered.

"I don't see a need and if I did, where would the pipes go? I'm miles away from any city, and that's how I like it."

"Such a hermit, Benny Bunny..." Jack teased. Ben glared back, but Nick knew it was deeply rooted brotherly love.

"Okay, that's enough. Thank you, Ben. Did you have any entreaties?"

"Just a request. When I send a letter with one of my hawks, will you please provide a resting place for them before they return? I had one return so worn out a few months back it took weeks to nurse it back to full health." Ben had spent generations training and breeding Ferruginous hawks to deliver messages. Modern technology rendered them unnecessary, but he continued. His loyalty to the animals was matched only by their loyalty to him. Ben took his seat and Kaida stood to take her turn.

CHAPTER 7

Kaida's gait was elegant and sure. Her beauty turned heads, but her demeanor demanded respect. She stood at the front, holding her stack of papers. As she opened her mouth to speak, Allie squeaked out, "Congratulations on the election!"

"Thank you, Allie." Kaida's smile was warm, but then a flicker of exhaustion crossed her face. The protectors withstood the illnesses of this earth. They didn't tire as easily as mortals, making sleep and food less essential, but still necessary. Nick found that his mind would tire well before his body, making sleep a pleasant reprieve.

Kaida had worked tirelessly, campaigning for Senator Inez this past year. Kaida excelled in campaigns and politics. She knew the strengths of the candidates and knew who would be most beneficial to the protector's missions and truly helpful to the people of earth. The most heartbreaking scene was a poor leader, or one consumed with malice. Good people can do terrible things under the rule of a corrupt leader.

"Senator Inez promoted me to chief of staff. My schedule will be incredibly busy beginning in the new year." She mentioned her packed schedule in almost every council. "I'll be able to be in the thick of policy making and important votes that affect not only the United States but the world. There is so much corruption in government agencies and political offices. It's nice to be at a central location where I can hear the news and we can all stay ahead of the crises. I will serve in that role this year and be living in Washington D.C., close to the White House. Though I'm rarely home."

Nick could attest to that. On various occasions, Kaida had needed help from him or vice versa and he'd waited for hours, sometimes days, at her home before getting to talk to her. The sound of a tapping foot interrupted his thoughts. He looked around the room to see Ben moving rhythmically in his seat. What was his rush? His face was flushed. If the protectors got sick, he would think Ben was coming down with something. They'd all seen sickness, but never experienced it themselves. It made them better helpers, especially in plagues and pandemics, or in poorer areas of the world where vaccines to the basic illnesses were not accessible. Ben's agitation seemed to be more than just the claustrophobia of being inside. Nick resolved to catch him after counsel and ask.

"I have entreaties for Nick, Jack, and Allie. If you are willing. Nick, I was discussing with Ben earlier a political agenda brought to the U.S. government. They are advertising it as a help to the environment, but it is just about politics and power. If passed it will do more harm than good and the only people that will benefit will be a few specific companies that have already agreed to build the technologies required. There seems to be one man slightly more invested than others. I don't think we can reach him, but his son, who is his confidant and business partner, could help. If we can convince him to do the right thing, then the bill might not pass.

"No," Nick said, clasping his hand around his pen, a flare of anger rising in his gut.

"No?" Kaida said, looking as if Nick had slapped her. She cleared her throat and assumed her professional persona. "I'm sorry. Of course, you are busy. I can find another way. I just thought…"

"No," Nick said, softer this time. "It's not my schedule. I will not give a thought to a man who will most likely ignore and disregard it." Kaida's features relaxed as realization dawned.

"We'll have to find a different way," she said.

"Yes, it is so much easier to give confidence or feed a flame of passion than it is to change a vengeful, selfish mind. I cannot change free will. That is the Creator's gift to all humankind, even when they abuse it," Nick said. Everyone nodded their agreement.

"I will look among those who are against this specific bill and find someone who needs the encouragement to rally against it. There are always people on both sides of the argument. I'll reach out when I find someone. Thank you, Nick." He nodded and released the grip he held on his pen. "Jack, regarding this political bill, there is a meeting..." Kaida went into a detailed plan of how Jack could use the weather to subdue an influential member in the political campaign dead set on seeing the bill passed.

"That sounds fun," Jack said, rubbing his hands together. "It's always a joy to see the looks on people's faces when the weather suddenly shifts." Nick exhaled a laugh. Jack was always up to some sort of lighthearted mischief, often targeting Ben. Of course, he'd be more than willing to cause mischief for a noble purpose.

"I hope that if we can delay him, I can give my statement before he gets his hooks in the minds of the opponents." The competitive gleam in Kaida's eye was not unfamiliar to this group. She gave a nod and turned to Allie. "That being said, if you know of any laws or similar cases from the past that could be beneficial, I'd appreciate any help." A ripping sound came from his right and Nick looked over to see Allie tearing a page from her notebook. She held it out for Kaida.

"These are a few off the top of my head. I wrote their reference numbers and where to find them." Nick glimpsed the paper as it traded hands. There had to be at least ten references on it.

"How..." Kaida began.

"I thought of a few as soon as you mentioned the political agenda. I wrote them down just in case."

"Thank you. This will save a lot of time."

"Be sure to read, or have your assistant read, the case from 2002. Very similar to what you're dealing with and a very solid case where the government did not win."

"Sounds perfect." Kaida tucked the paper somewhere inside her cloak.

"The last thing I wished to discuss..." Kaida's words vanished as a harsh wind picked up, tightly wrapping her golden cloak around her slight frame. The notebook pages and papers on Nick's desk fluttered, and he reflexively threw an arm down to stop them from blowing away. He felt the temperature in the room drop and had just enough time to look at Jack. His friend had his hand raised, causing the wind to blow over him instead of directly at him like everyone else. If it wasn't Jack, then who? No sooner had he thought this than a voice icier than the room pierced his heart.

"I will be released. Be prepared. I am coming."

A laugh echoed off the walls and seemed to swirl around the room on the fine black dust that now filled the air, and then it was gone. All that remained was the black dust settling on almost every surface of the room. All the protectors were on their feet, each with their staff in hand. Nick's heart pounded as he stood frozen in place. His fight response surged through him, but the threat was gone. He forced his shoulder muscles to relax as he turned to the stern faces and wide eyes of his friends.

"The Shadow." Ben's whisper felt loud in the silent room.

CHAPTER 8

"I have to go," Ben said, kicking back his chair. It rolled and hit the wall. He rushed to the door without glancing back.

"Wait! We need to discuss this," Kaida said authoritatively, her hands shaking slightly.

"There's nothing to discuss. We all knew this day would come. We need to be prepared, and that's exactly what I plan to do." With one surreptitious glance and a turn on his heel, he was gone. They heard a door out of the Time Room slam.

"What do we do?" Allie asked in a shaky voice, turning to Nick.

"Let him go. He's had something on his mind since the moment he got here," Nick answered.

"Not about him. About the Shadow," she said, exasperated. Nick placed an elbow on his desk and rubbed his forehead.

"For now, there isn't much we can do. We know he is still bound, but his warning could be just a threat."

"He's never contacted us before," Kaida said. "How does he have that power?"

"He feeds on the chaos of this world and the malice of men. We all brought up concerns about the world's overall health decreasing. He will only become stronger because of it."

"Can we take any preemptive actions?" Kaida asked, her political voice and stance at the ready.

"I'm open to suggestions." Nick looked around at the other three, but no one had any ideas. The shock was still too fresh. Nick exhaled loudly. "Continue on as you are now, but let's keep our eyes and ears open. Let's council again in eight weeks and we can discuss how things have progressed."

"Or digressed," Jack muttered under his breath. The darkness of his statement sunk deep into Nick's chest.

"Can someone get a note to Ben? It's usually easy to catch one of his hawks outside the New Zealand Library," Nick said.

"I will," Allie volunteered as everyone gathered their notes. "I think they like me best. If he's heading home, then I bet it will catch him along the path." She shrugged. "I'll take it after I clean up this mess," she said, running her pointer finger along her desk, leaving a line in the black dust.

"You take the note. I'd like to clean up. I could use the time to think, and I don't have to leave for my flight for a few hours," Nick said. Allie's tense stance and furrowed brow told Nick she would rather get home.

"I moved the cleaning supplies to the right shelf in the closet when I reorganized." Nick nodded, and Allie followed Jack from the room.

"My schedule is full, but I will clear space for the next meeting." Kaida said with a wave, leaving the council room. Her heels clicked against the floor with each quick step.

Nick remained seated, leaning back in his office chair, staring at the wall. He allowed his mind to relax. He felt guilty for not telling the others, but he believed it for the best. As he heard the voice of the Shadow, his eyes were closed and, in the darkness, he saw himself as if a bird, flying over forests, rivers, and mountains, to a cave. He saw a few defining markers in his mind–a waterfall, a knotted tree, three stones along the trail, and an overgrown path. Just inside the cave, he saw a boar. It paced the entry of the cave and as Nick approached the cave in his vision, it turned, its glowing red eyes glared into his own. He somehow knew the beast could see him. The vision ended as quickly as it started, and while it felt like a long journey in his mind, it lasted only moments and ended with the Shadow's chilling laugh. His mind now held a map to the cave that held the Shadow captive.

He'd seen the glowing eyes of the beast that held the Shadow. Why? What reason would the beast have to share its location with him? Why not the others? As a group, minus Ben, they'd concluded that the Shadow's powers must be getting stronger as he fed off the growing darkness of the world. His mind spun around these unanswered questions as he gathered the cleaning supplies and got to work. Over an hour later, he returned the broom and dustpan to the closet, gathered his duffle bag, shoulder bag, and staff, and left the council room. A harsh rustling to his right brought him to an abrupt stop.

"Hello?" he called, his voice echoing off the Time Room walls. He thought everyone had left after council. A door slammed straight across the room from him, but the globe blocked his view. He dropped the duffle bag and ran around to the other side. They could've exited through one of three doors: New Zealand, China, or the Cayman Islands. He walked back around the way he'd come to retrieve his bag. He froze, his gaze drawn to the restricted shelf. The metal bar sealing the forbidden books was broken.

CHAPTER 9

Nick's heart pounded as he saw the damage done to the shelf. The metal had been twisted back and away from the books, and the soft golden glow that shielded the shelf was gone. His eyes scanned the books frantically. He had paid little attention to this shelf, knowing that its contents were forbidden. There didn't seem to be anything missing, except... Nick's eyes narrowed in on a book with its top corner tipped back, not fully settled on the shelf. His hand hovered over the disturbed book. Was he breaking the Creator's command by taking the book? Or was he doing his job as leader, finding out what was so important that one of his friends would risk the Creator's displeasure? His hand dropped to his side as he considered the consequences. He turned his back and walked a lap around the Time Room, taking long measured strides. Did the risk of taking the book outweigh the risk of not knowing what knowledge was stolen? He stared at the damaged shelf, then back to the book. Nick slowly raised his arm and removed the worn book from the shelf. He parted his cloak and placed the book in the bag slung across his shoulder. He needed to catch a plane.

Nick left the Time Room through the door to the Rosebank library in Johannesburg. He paused. In his rush, he'd forgotten to look at the time above the door before entering. He listened and couldn't hear or feel anyone close and one glance out the library window showed why. The sun was just beginning to rise over the mountains. The library was not open yet. It had been a few years since he had entered this library and he had to wrack his memory. Was there a safe exit? Was he going to set off alarms? No, not at this library. No alarms, just a security guard. Nick glanced around the bookshelf and still only saw an empty library. He walked carefully around the bookshelf, past the check-out desk, and approached the front door. The door had been locked from the inside. He quickly unlocked the deadbolt and entered the quiet street. Nick walked away from the library toward where he thought he might find a taxi driver. A man in a black waterproof coat, dark sunglasses and black hat with a security logo walked toward him with a cup of something hot, taking a bite out of a piece of jam covered toast. The security guard's head raised, and he quickly swallowed and brought the toast away from his face.

The man spoke loudly in a language Nick couldn't understand, Tsonga perhaps. Nick nodded politely, but the man approached him, speaking loudly and pointing toward the library. Nick shrugged nonchalantly, shuffling his staff to his other arm so he could point to his ears with another shrug. He hurried around the security guard and darted into an alley between two buildings. The security guard didn't follow, so he must have determined that Nick was not a threat. He slung his duffle bag over his back and broke into a jog, just in case the guard changed his mind after seeing that the library door was unlocked.

He exited the alley and found a taxi driver asleep in his cab further down the road. Nick wrapped his knuckles on the window to wake him. The driver jumped and unlocked his doors. Nick said 'airport' in both English and German, hoping the word was at least similar to one that the driver would understand. The driver repeated the word in English and moved his hand through the air to indicate a flying plane. Nick was relieved by the understanding. He knew that, at least, the airport workers would all speak English and he reflected on the usefulness of Kaida's gift of languages, as he usually did in these situations.

He paid the taxi driver, leaving a generous tip for interrupting his sleep, then headed into the airport. He checked the duffle bag, then followed the signs to security. The line was short at this time of day. He stood behind two men who looked to be traveling for business. He took the time to breathe. There were few places as stressful as airports; even the calmest souls felt anxious and rushed inside an airport. Nick knew the constant struggle of pushing those emotions away from himself, almost like a mental shield, in order to maintain his calm demeanor and keep his heart rate steady.

A security agent became available, and he pulled his passport and ticket from his bag. He'd printed the ticket at the library in New York before entering the Time Room to meditate.

"Mr. Smith?" the Transportation Security Officer asked without a smile, flipping through Nick's passport. "So well-traveled, yes?" Nick nodded and reached for his passport. The man directed him to a line where he could send his shoulder bag through the scanners. The first time that Nick had flown, he wasn't sure what to do with his staff. It was always with him, and he didn't want to send it through the scanners. So, he'd kept it with him and in the hundreds of years that he's flown since not a single person had mentioned it. He assumed that, like his cloak, it was disguised as something else, or maybe not visible at all. He was grateful to not part with it in such a busy place. It was a constant in his ever moving, ever changing life. He felt stronger, more focused, with his staff in his hand.

Once through security, he settled into a chair by the gate to wait. The ancient book nagged at him, insisting that he satiate his curiosity. He was about to reach his hand into his cloak to retrieve the book, but a light pressure on his knee interrupted him. He looked up from his bag and down into the big brown eyes of a young toddler, whose perfect little fingers and palm were resting on his knee. Where had she come from? She looked up at him with bright, curious eyes and a finger in her mouth. Nick looked around to see if any panic-stricken parents were looking for her.

When his search turned up empty, he looked down to see the girl's head tilted, her eyebrows scrunched, still sucking on her finger. He offered a small smile, and she reached her arms up toward him. Once again, he looked around, but there was no one searching for the child. He gently lifted her into his lap and she put her finger back in her mouth, her gaze still on Nick's face. She reached out her hand that wasn't in her mouth and touched his beard. He softly gasped and spun his head to look at the girl. She giggled and ran her hand over his face. The moisture on her hand didn't concern him. Children's hands were always wet or sticky or cold or all three. When her tiny hand reached his nose, he shook his head, pretending to dodge her fingers, making her giggle more around the finger in her mouth. They played that game for another few minutes before she ducked her head and cuddled into Nick's chest.

"We'd better find your parent, young one," Nick said, standing. He balanced the girl on his side with one arm underneath her. He didn't want to make a scene at security if he could find the girl's parents or guardian on his own. His boarding gate was the last along the corridor, so he assumed she'd come from the other direction. He reached out to the surrounding emotions to find the intense gut-wrenching panic of someone who had lost their child, but couldn't find any. Odd. Whoever was missing the girl must be unaware. He could feel the tired lethargy of many passengers as they came off planes or waited for theirs to land so they could load and make it to their early morning destination. Nick was about to turn to the security desk, having not found anyone looking for the child, when the girl suddenly lunged sideways in his arms.

"Dad, da, da," she said, pointing and reaching. Nick set her down, and she toddled over to a man slumped back in his chair, sound asleep. The little girl attempted to climb into the chair next to the man. Nick now understood why there wasn't any panic. The man appeared to be alone and was clearly exhausted. He looked at the clock on the wall. His flight wouldn't board for another twenty minutes. He sat two seats from the man and pulled the girl into his lap again. He could let the wearied parent rest for a few more minutes. Sleep may be the man's only relief from a troubling situation. He entertained the girl by facing her toward him and clapping her hands together, then placing her own hands over her eyes and beginning a game of peekaboo. Suddenly, the man sat up straight, his eyes flying open, and Nick felt the panic that he'd been expecting earlier.

"Mia," the man's voice was raspy from his unexpected nap. He looked around the ground frantically before looking up and seeing the girl giggling in Nick's lap.

"I'm so sorry, sir," the man said in a thick accent. He reached for the girl and she wiggled down from Nick's lap and ran to him. Nick knew they had found the right person.

"It's no trouble. What a wonderful, curious child you have." Nick was happy to relieve the man's panic and have him believe the girl had only wandered a few seats over, not to a different gate entirely.

"She gets that from her mother. She was always wanting to learn and explore." Nick didn't miss the past tense or the heaviness of his words. "I can't believe I dozed off. It makes me sick thinking about what could've happened."

"She was perfectly safe."

"Yes, yes, well, thank you." He squeezed one arm tightly around his daughter, while the other rubbed the sleep from his eyes.

"You can do this," Nick said. The father looked at him skeptically. "You *can* do this," Nick said again firmly.

"Thank you," the father said, tears gathering in his eyes. Nick pushed away his own emotions and those of everyone around and focused on this heartbroken young father. He clasped a hand on the man's shoulder and transferred one word. *Peace.*

In the desperation of whatever this man's situation, he knew the father would latch on and find peace. Despite his broken heart, he would heal. Mia would help. He had someone to be strong for. The agent at his counter announced his plane was now boarding. He nodded to the man and returned swiftly to his gate. He lined up with the others and silently thanked the Creator for allowing him to help this broken family, if only for one moment in their rough journey ahead.

As he found his seat on the plane, he was glad to see that the flight was only half full and everyone would have a little extra elbow room. Despite the accumulated wealth of the protectors, he still preferred to live and travel frugally. They could use the money better elsewhere. He unlatched his cloak in order to take his bag off and place it under the seat in front of him. He fastened his cloak as quickly as he could and settled back into his seat. Living for hundreds of years will help you develop patience, but Nick was feeling it tested as his curiosity about the book heightened.

Finally, their plane was in the air, and their long flight was underway. The fasten seatbelt sign was switched off, and he pulled the worn brown book from his bag. He gently opened it, both because of the integrity of the ancient book and the sacred nature. The symbols and writing on the page were unfamiliar to him - Sanskrit, perhaps? Maybe something else. His first thought was that Kaida could read it, his second was that perhaps Allie would know. Flipping through the ancient pages, he attempted to make sense of the unfamiliar symbols and writing. He continued studying the pages as the hours of flight time passed. The crew brought lunch, and he set the book aside to eat his slightly stale ham sandwich and chips. Picking the book up, he opened it to where he'd marked it with the fraying ribbon bookmarker. As he turned toward the second half of the book, a few pages flipped together, opening to a torn page. The symbols and words at the top of the page remained, but someone had removed the bottom half. Had the Creator removed this page before putting it on the sealed shelf? Or did the one who didn't want to be caught in the Time Room remove it? Either way, why this page? What was the significance? Nick closed the book harder than intended in his frustration. The woman across the aisle jumped and then glared at him for interrupting her own reading. He slid the book gently back into his bag and sat back, taking a few deep breaths.

A lot had happened in the past few hours and yet, not much had changed. He was still needed at the displacement camp; the Shadow was still bound, this book which he could not read was no more unread than it was for the rest of Nick's long life, and yet everything felt different. It was as though the world itself were on the edge of a cliff and any sudden shift would send it careening into a freefall so long and deep that there would be no recovery.

He had a mission to complete in Ethiopia, then he'd be free to figure this out. The protectors were meeting in a few weeks and he'd be able to get help with translation that he needed to even know what the book was about. While he could not read the words, he could feel a sort of ominous power within it. Perhaps that was just his knowledge of its forbidden nature. Nick leaned his head back on the plane seat and closed his eyes, the soothing sound of the plane's engine rumbling in the background.

CHAPTER 10
ENLAND 1848

Nick sat on the steps of the orphanage, his elbows resting on his knees, an eight-inch crooked knife in hand. He had whittled away at this piece of birch wood for the past few days and was happy with the results. It was a small soldier, in the image of a Queen's Guard with a tall bearskin hat and a sash crossed in front of its stiff tunic. The small toy fit nicely in his hand. He found that having something to do with his hands helped ease the strain and heavy emotions of the financial depression sweeping the world. Unemployment rates were astronomically high, families were struggling, and sickness was widespread, with no extra money to spend on doctors.

The worst part of the depression was seeing the children. Their innocent minds were too young to understand finances, but they understood hunger. They understood parents arguing, and they picked up on emotions around them almost as easily as Nick could. He made his last cut in the wood and admired his work.

"Keep up, keep up, children," a cheerful voice called. "We can't be late, it's almost time for Bible study." A group of a few dozen children trundled in front of Nick's waiting place. They walked together in a tight group, most likely because of the icy temperatures. The long sleeve dresses worn by the young girls, either a brown or dark gray, hung almost to the ground. White short-sleeved aprons covered the dresses. The older boys wore black trousers and black jackets, with a white collar standing up stiffly around their necks. They wore tall socks and thick shoes. A coverall apron crossed the boy's chests and went down past their waist.

The voice belonged to a woman in a thick dark dress with a shawl wrapped around her shoulders. Her sharp features and straight nose gave her a fierce look, but her soft voice resonated with kindness. The children's readiness to follow her lead shared more of the character of this woman than anything else in Nick's mind. As the woman noticed Nick on the stairs, she straightened.

"Good day, sir, you must be here to see Mr. Muller."

"I am. Are you a volunteer at this establishment?" he asked. The woman opened the door into the house and stood holding it open as the children entered. He could see two women inside, dressed in dark dresses with long white aprons tied around their waists, ushering kids in, ready to help with the transition from the cold outdoors.

"Each of you remove your coats and place them appropriately in your rooms. Change into your nightgowns and prepare for Bible study," she implored loudly before she turned back to Nick. "A volunteer? Yes, I suppose I am," she said with a happy gleam in her eye. "I am Mrs. Muller, but you may call me Mary."

"Of course, Mary. I see you are busy. I will wait here and stay out of the way until Mr. Muller returns or you are less busy."

"Sir, we are always busy. So many children to tend to. If you are to wait for a non-busy moment, you'd grow old right here on this step. Please come inside where it's warm." Nick shuffled in after the last of the children and, as he did, his eyes settled on a small boy at the edge of the entryway. He looked to be about seven or eight and he stood as if in a stupor. His hands went through the motions of removing the blanket from his shoulders, but his eyes remained unfocused. Nick pushed aside the collective emotions of all the children to focus on this boy. Grief and displacement fought to devour this young child. All the other children had gone off to their rooms to change, but the boy still stood in the hallway. Mary finished giving directions to one of the older children to help with a younger one when she turned around and spotted the boy.

"James, dearest." She walked over and gently took the blanket from him. "After we go for a walk, it is time to change into nightgowns and prepare for Bible study." The boy looked at Mary, his eyes blank and staring.

"Yes, ma'am," he mumbled. He followed up the stairs in the same direction the other boys had gone. Mary watched with eyes filled with sympathy before turning to her guest.

"Mr.... I don't recall your name."

"You may call me Nick, as we are to be on a first name basis," he smiled warmly. "Can you tell me about young James? He seems so downtrodden."

"Yes, the poor lad," Mary said, folding the boy's blanket, draping it over her arm, and holding it close to her. "He came to us less than two weeks ago. According to the neighbors that dropped him here, his father took off when he lost his job, as many men did. They'd rather leave than see their families starve, and unfortunately, that's exactly what happened. His mother didn't have enough to eat, opting to give anything she had to the boy and his sister. She took ill and passed, as did the sister. It all happened very quickly. The neighbors expressed their regrets at not being able to keep him, but they, like almost everyone, were struggling just to feed their own children. He has spoken little since he got here and mentally seems to be in a different place altogether."

"Poor soul." Nick's heart broke for the boy.

"Yes, many children come to us in this state. We do our best to nurture and uplift. Eventually, they'll come out of their shell and interact with the others, but they will never be as carefree or lively as other children. There is just too much pain. They learn to grow up so fast," Mary said.

"I understand," Nick said, clearing his throat, his chest tight with emotion. He knew the Creator had directed him here, to England, to find George Muller. It was becoming very clear to him why. "When is Mr. Muller expected to return?" Nick inquired, his curiosity growing.

"He moves on the Lord's errand in everything he does. He typically arrives here at this time to read the Bible with the children, but if he prays and feels he is needed elsewhere, then that is where he will go. I don't mind doing the reading."

"Such dedication is admirable." Just as the words left his mouth, the door opened behind him and a man, looking to be nearing fifty, entered.

His shoulders were hunched against the cold, but he had the bounce in his step of a much younger man. He removed his hat, showing dark hair with plenty of gray hairs peppered throughout. He hung the hat on the decorative end of the banister leading upstairs.

"Mary, have I made it in time to read? You will not believe the goodness of God I witnessed today..." the man stopped abruptly, noticing Nick. "Oh, hello Sir. I don't believe we've met."

"I'm Nick," he said, extending his hand.

"Nick, short for Nicholas?" the man asked, releasing Nick's hand. He spoke with a slight German accent, his eyes somehow jolly. Nick just gave a tight-lipped smile, and the man hurried on. "I'm George Muller, and it seems you've met my wife Mary already." He gave his wife a quick peck on the cheek.

"Yes, it's been my pleasure," Nick said with a slight bow. As he straightened, he caught sight of himself in the round mirror next to the door. His reflection showed a middle-class style. He observed a black-collared coat with a buttoned off-white vest beneath it before returning his attention to the Mullers.

"You are just in time to read; the children are changing. I'm on my way to help now," Mary said to Mr. Muller, taking the first few steps before turning back to ask, "Have you had anything to eat?"

"I'll eat after reading. Thank you, dear."

"I apologize for the timing," Mr. Muller said to Nick. "I must read to the children. After that, my time is all yours to discuss whatever has brought you to us on this fine cold day. Would you care to join us?"

"I'd be honored," Nick said, and he followed Mr. Muller into a room with a threadbare rug thrown across the wooden floor. There were rocking chairs in two of the corners. The fire had a large grate around it and glowed as it filled the room with a comfortable warmth and flickering light. Children's drawings covered almost every inch of the walls. Mr. Muller sat in one rocking chair and pointed to the other, indicating that Nick should sit down.

"The women will be in shortly with the children, once the little ones are all in their nightgowns. We like to end the day with the Lord's words. Are you a religious man, Nick?"

"I feel an intimate connection with the Creator, so yes, I believe you'd say I was." The sound of running feet caused both men to turn. The rumble of little feet on the stairs reminded Nick of just how many children were being housed in this small building.

A young boy entered the room first, running as fast as his little legs could carry him. He dashed straight to Mr. Muller's knee. The boy, about three years old, raised his arms and Mr. Muller scooped him into his lap with a laugh.

"I first," he said with a satisfied grin.

"You certainly are! Those feet of yours grow stronger and faster every day." Mr. Muller said, poking the boy in his side and getting the sweetest giggle in return. The boy laid his head back against Mr. Muller's chest. Nick's heart warmed at the scene. He could see that Mr. Muller's reputation was not exaggerated.

One by one, the children filed in and found a place to sit on the floor. The older children seemed to have favorite places around the fire. The women came in last, with a child clinging to each hand.

"Mr. Nick, it seems I am not going anywhere," he gazed adoringly at the boy in his lap. "Would you mind handing me that Bible from the mantle, please?" Mr. Muller pointed above the fireplace. Nick stood and offered his seat to the closest volunteer, who took it gratefully.

Nick picked the book off the mantle with one hand. Its cover was soft and it curved against his fingers. This was well-worn, and he looked forward to hearing the words in Mr. Muller's deep voice and German accent.

"Thank you. Please, have a seat wherever you can find space," Mr. Muller said lightheartedly. Nick was careful not to step on any fingers or toes as he navigated toward the back of the room. His eyes landed on little James and he found a seat next to the boy. Mr. Muller read, and Nick watched as James picked at a thread coming loose from the rug. For the first few minutes, the children sat quietly, but as the reading continued, they began to squirm and become restless. Mr. Muller sensed the change and started asking questions. What did they think of the scripture? Did they understand a certain word? What is an example of this scripture in real life? The children were excited to raise their hands, even the younger ones that had paid little attention at all. Mr. Muller was patient with their nonsensical answers and always found a way to make it the right answer.

Nick watched James continue to pick at the rug string. He twirled it around his small finger, let it go, and wound it up again. He didn't raise his hand to answer any of the questions and never looked up from the rug. After a few more minutes of discussion, the volunteers took the children to bed. The older kids led the way, a few of them with children on their hips, and the volunteers followed behind. Nick stood against the wall and watched the children head up the stairs.

"The most excellent time of day," Mr. Muller said with a sigh. Nick didn't ask whether he meant bedtime or Bible study. "Come with me. We can talk in my office." The rocking chair creaked lightly as Mr. Muller stood. He led Nick to a small room down the hallway on the first floor. There was a wooden desk in the middle of the room with only just enough space for Mr. Muller to squeeze around it. Nick sat in the wooden chair across from Mr. Muller. A single letter on the desk caught his attention, but Mr. Muller picked it up quickly and shoved it into a drawer.

"Now, what can I do for you, Mr. Nick?"

"I have a donation," Nick said, getting right to the point. Mr. Muller's eyes grew wide and then misty.

"Thank you," he said in a hoarse voice. "The Lord never ceases to bless these orphans. He sends his servants just as he sees a need." Nick knew this to be true and nodded his agreement. Mr. Muller opened a desk drawer and shuffled through, pulling out a slip of paper. He set it in front of him on the desk and picked up his pen.

"How much shall I write down, sir?"

"I wish for the donation to remain anonymous," Nick said sternly. Mr. Muller set down his pen and looked Nick in the eye.

"I'm afraid that's not possible."

"I must insist." Nick said in his same stern tone. Mr. Muller crossed his arms in front of him, weighing his answer. He opened another drawer and pulled out a stack of papers, identical to the one he'd begun filling out for Nick. He dropped them down on the desk between them.

"No. *I* must insist," Mr. Muller said. "I record every farthing given to the orphanages. Many men have come in to make their donations anonymous and I respect that. I will not breathe a word to anyone. Only you, I, and the good Lord will know what is written here," Mr. Muller assured. Nick looked at the determined look on his face and changed tactics.

"I have a large donation, and I wish it to not be recorded," Nick said, leaning back and crossing his arms.

"Let me tell you a story." Mr. Muller said, leaning back and matching Nick's body language. This announcement surprised Nick, but he settled in to listen. "There was once a young lad, raised in a home of faith. He had a mother and father that loved him and raised him right. Unfortunately, when this boy hit adolescence, he fell in with the wrong crowd. He rebelled against the principles that he had lived and adhered to in his parents' home. He gained a reputation for himself. Not a good one, I might add," he paused and looked at Nick before continuing.

"This boy drank and gambled. He spent time with women in ways disgraceful to his and their reputations. It began innocently enough, but spiraled out of control quickly. He couldn't satiate his worldly lusts. When this boy couldn't afford to pay for a hotel he had stayed at, he was thrown into prison until he settled his debts, which served as a wake-up call for him. He spent thirty days in a cell. Plenty of time to think over his actions and wish for better things for himself. His father bailed him out, and he returned home. Despite the desire to change, the flesh was weak and the boy quickly returned to his sinful ways. His father cut him off, no longer willing to support such behavior, as any good father should. This boy, unable to stop, began to steal. No one was safe from his deceit. He pickpocketed, ran backhanded schemes, and stole from even his closest friends. His second wake-up call came when his mother passed away." Mr. Muller paused and took a deep breath.

"This boy was at a gambling hall when his mother drew her last breath. They couldn't find him to alert him until the next day. Not that it would have done them any good the night of her death, as the boy was too deep into his drink to remember anything." He wiped at the corner of his eye. Nick felt the shame coming from Muller and there was no question about who this story was about. "The boy vowed to do better but was unsure how. He stumbled through and had many relapses until he had a university friend invite him to a Bible study group. The words and the Holy Spirit touched his heart and changed his course forever." Understanding dawned on Nick.

"As you can guess, or perhaps have already heard, that boy was me." Mr. Muller placed a hand on his chest and lowered his eyes. "I have come so far from that boy that the memories feel like those of someone else. But because of that past, you must understand. I will record and account for every dollar donated to the orphanages. My past will not dictate the reputation of this home. Everything must be and will be transparent, not a single discrepancy. Ever." He looked Nick in the eye and Nick sensed the man's remorse for his past behaviors, his gratitude for the life he lived now, and his determination on this matter.

"Thank you for explaining and sharing your story, Mr. Muller. I believe I understand," Nick said, thinking fast.

"Thank you for understanding, now..." Mr. Muller picked up his pen. "What is the last name for the order?"

"Smith." Nick blurted, the first name to come to his mind. He cleared his throat. "Nick Smith."

"An American surname," he said as a fact, not a question. "Not Nicholas?" Mr. Muller asked, eyebrows raised.

"No sir, just Nick, ending with a k."

"Very well, and the amount?" Nick pulled a stack of money from the bag beneath his cloak and placed it on the desk. Mr. Muller looked at it, shocked. He looked from Nick to the money on the desk multiple times. He again dropped his pen to the desk and leaned back.

"There is no mistake? This is for the orphanage?" Mr. Muller asked.

"Yes sir, every farthing," Nick answered. Mr. Muller placed a hand over his heart and looked upward.

"Again, the good Lord has provided an angel." He reached into his desk and pulled out the letter he had stuffed away when they entered the small office.

"I received a letter today. It's not the first of its kind. It is from a neighbor of the orphanage complaining about the noise of the children and the streets' inability to handle the number of people living here. The lines are becoming backed up. Mary and I have discussed building a new orphanage, a bigger one, on land outside of Bristol, but we do not have the funds. You have just given me hope and a start toward building that home. The economics of this era are challenging for many and there are still kids on the streets despite our best efforts. Thank you, Mr. Smith," Mr. Muller's gratitude was matched by Nick's. He was grateful to help in such an important cause. They stood and shook hands across the desk.

"Are you in a hurry to be off, or can I give you a tour of this home?"

Nick smiled at hearing him refer to it as a home and not an orphanage. He truly cared about the poor children.

"That would be wonderful. I'd love to see the logistics of taking care of this many children."

"It's no small feat." Mr. Muller laughed. "Right this way." Mr. Muller showed him the kitchen and bathing areas on the main floor, but didn't feel he had to show him the play room again, where they had done their Bible study. "Upstairs are the children's rooms. Girls on the left, boys on the right." He paused to listen outside the boy's room and then slowly opened the door. There was a volunteer tucking in the little boy that had jumped into Mr. Muller's lap earlier. His droopy eyes showed that sleep wasn't far away.

Once again, Nick found himself drawn to young James, whose bed was closest to the door. His eyes were closed, but Nick could feel the anxious energy and the squirm in the boy's stomach as though it were his own. Next to the boy's bed were his clothes, neatly folded, and his shoes lined up beside those. Mr. Muller went to talk to the volunteer and Nick reached into his bag. He felt the smooth wood of the recently finished soldier and withdrew it. Nick took a few steps over to James' bed and placed the toy soldier inside one of the boy's shoes. He cleared his mind and pushed out the emotions of everyone else and focused on James, who still pretended to sleep. Nick knew he wouldn't be able to take away the boy's grief, and he didn't want to. Grief shapes and strengthens us, it becomes a part of who we are. He placed a hand on the boy's arm and transferred the word *create*. Let young James take his grief and use it to create something beautiful. Let the act of creating give him a sense of relief from that grief. The boy stilled and opened one eye just a crack. Nick winked, and the boy quickly looked away and scrunched his eyes closed. Nick caught Mr. Muller's eye and the two of them left the boys' room, closing the door softly behind them.

"Thank you again for your generous donation, Nick. You can't imagine what it will mean for the work we are trying to do here," Mr. Muller said.

"Give the glory to the Creator. He led me to your doorstep and will continue helping you with your mission," Nick said reverently.

"God bless you, Nick," Mr. Muller said. He then surprised Nick by throwing his arms around him in a tight embrace before bidding him farewell.

CHAPTER 11

Nick jerked forward and felt his seat belt tighten across his lap. The pilot's static voice came over the intercom to announce their arrival. Nick would take a bus from the airport to the train station and from there meet Ajani, a humanitarian leader assigned to the displacement camp.

The dream he received reminded him that there were no coincidences. It was not a coincidence that Nick was helping a family in Germany when he overheard others talking about a German that had done a great work of establishing orphanages in England. It piqued his curiosity and then everywhere he went he heard more whisperings, more discussions, about a George Muller - the German that saved children from the harsh streets of England.

Nick wondered what had happened to that young boy, James. Although, now it would be hard to know, he'd grown old and returned to the Creator by now. That was the way with a lot of souls Nick had been sent to help. He helped where the Creator called him and then left, trusting them to His care.

As the plane landed, Nick threw his bag over his shoulder and followed the line of people to the boarding bridge. He watched his steps, maneuvering around people on the gangplank, but looked up as he felt the rush of cool air from inside the airport. His eyes immediately went to a large sign on the wall straight ahead of him. It was a picture of a jolly Santa Claus with a bag slung over his shoulder, the name 'Yágena Abāt', in bold print across the bottom. Even in a country where gift giving isn't a big part of the Christmas tradition, the westernized St. Nicholas still had a presence here. He was glad to be spending this Christmas helping at the camp instead of surrounded by the commercialism of the season.

Nick followed the signs and arrows to collect his checked duffle bag and then to the buses. He found one, headed to the train station, and boarded. Once there, he purchased his ticket and waited for the train to arrive. He found a bench and settled his duffle bag next to him on the ground. He looked forward to gifting these. They were very needed.

People filed past, heads down, as they went to different areas of the station. A monotone voice sounded over the intercom, listing the times and destinations of the next few trains. There were business people in suits, men in t-shirts with threads hanging from the sleeves, mothers in long dresses with babies wrapped in bundles in slings on their backs, youth sleeping with their heads on backpacks. Nick kept his head up and observed. Occasionally, he'd channel into someone's emotions, just to see if their body language matched their feelings. The waiting and the train ride seemed short as he weighed his feelings about the ancient book in his bag. He'd thought about opening it again on the train but couldn't yet bring himself to do it. Was he at odds with the Creator's desire by taking the book, or was it a part of the plan? Only someone powerful could've taken the book. Nick imagined that one of their staffs would be the only thing strong enough to break the seal. But why? The timing just felt too coincidental. The Shadow's voice was heard in council, and then someone broke the seal on the same day. Nick exited the train, feeling unsettled. His attention diverted when he saw a man with dark skin and dark hair tipped in white, a retreating hairline showing his age. He held a cardboard sign with Nick's name written on it in pencil. The man looked right at Nick with a smile that lit up his entire face. Nick felt more at ease knowing that he'd found his guide and that he had such a positive energy about him.

"You must be Ajani?"

"Nick?" Ajani smiled and took his hand in a firm grip. "Thank you so much for coming. I am to pick you up and then gather some medical volunteers from the bus stop. Let us go," Ajani said enthusiastically. Nick had to concentrate on understanding his English through his thick accent, but was pleased to have found Ajani so easily. Ajani took Nick's black bag from him, staggering slightly under the weight, and led the way to a beat-up brown truck. Ajani threw Nick's bag into the back of the truck and climbed into the driver's seat. The passenger side Nick slid into didn't have a headrest. The middle console of the truck looked like it had been torn up by some kind of animal, and the windshield was challenging to see through because of all the dust. With a couple of tries, the engine roared to life, and they were off.

"You are from America, yes?" Ajani asked, his voice raised over the roar of the engine and the wind blowing through the open windows.

"I travel a lot of my time. You could say America is my home base," Nick agreed.

"We are so glad you are here, so glad. We will go pick up the medical volunteers and then go to camp. Hopefully, we can make it before dark." They pulled up to a bus stop and waited in the car. Nick found out about Ajani's four kids and wife. War casualties claimed the lives of his wife and two of their children. The other kids had grown up and were living in other countries. Ajani was a genuine leader, helping in any way possible, including coordinating relief efforts with global agencies and bringing volunteers like Nick and the medical teams.

He heard the bus before it puttered into view. Nick was no mechanic, but you didn't have to know much to be skeptical of the reliability of the bus pulling in to the stop. Its brakes let out a loud long squeak and release as the doors opened and people filed out. A group of young adults gathered to the side of the road. They had a few bags each, a few with red crosses on the front. Ajani got out of the truck and approached them. He shook hands with a man, most likely the medical team leader, and gestured toward his truck. Nick didn't have to count to know they wouldn't all fit in the truck's cab. He exited the passenger seat and climbed into the bed of the truck, pushing his bag to the back and using it as a seat. The medical volunteers took a few moments playing the 'who's going to sit up front' game, no one wanting to accept special treatment. In the end, a married couple - Nick assumed they were married because of their matching silicone rings, and the feelings of adoration and respect that he could feel they had for each other - climbed into the cab next to Ajani. They fit as many bags as they could into the cab, and then the rest of the medical team joined Nick in the back of the truck. It seemed unlikely that the truck would be able to drive with the added weight of the passengers and their bags.

Despite Nick's doubt, the truck roared to life, and they took a main road through town for a few miles before turning off onto a dirt road. Ajani drove his truck like it was a high-end off-road vehicle. As they traveled further from town, he flew over rocks and splashed through small streams. Nick and the other medical volunteers learned quickly to duck around branches and brace themselves against small boulders. Ajani had to pull over on narrow roads to let other vehicles squeeze past. They wound through mountains and hills for hours.

A poor medical student was clearly susceptible to motion sickness, and they all made room for him to lie down with his knees tucked into his chest. He only got up once to be sick over the side of the truck. Nick could feel the poor boy's discomfort tinged with embarrassment. He was sure this was not how he imagined his first day in Ethiopia going.

Everyone else brimmed with excitement and anticipation. Everyone in the truck would feel a fleeting flash of fear whenever Ajani took a turn too fast or hit a large bump in the road. However, the excitement of their shared adventure would quickly overpower and extinguish it. This group of young doctors were eager to use their medical knowledge to help these refugees. A more talkative volunteer, with red hair and braces attempted to start conversations a few times, but the noise of the truck and the rough terrain made more than a few words impossible and half the volunteers missed the answers so they settled into a comfortable silence. Nick gathered that the six volunteers in the back with him were students at a medical university in northern Africa, a few days' travel from Ethiopia. The two squished into the cab with Ajani and as many bags as possible were the leaders and coordinated all the volunteers, travel, and supplies.

After the first hour, they stopped apologizing to each other when their shoulders bumped or they were accidentally knocked off balance into another person. They just helped each other readjust and settled back into the comfortable silence of the uncomfortable ride.

The sun was low in the sky when the terrain turned from mountainous to desert. They could see the mountains behind them, but only dry dirt and sagebrush as far as they could see in front. The truck followed the divots in the dirt path created by other vehicles, or perhaps just this one, traveling to and from their destination. Eyes were heavy, and the sun was all but gone when they rolled into the camp. Fires illuminated several groupings of white tents, most with national emergency agency logos printed on the sides.

Ajani parked the truck and they all unloaded themselves and their bags from the back of the truck. The camp was quiet, as though its tenants had settled down for the night. He could hear the wind rustling the tents and an infant crying in the distance.

"I will lead you to your tent tonight and will give you a tour of the camp tomorrow," Ajani said, stifling a yawn. There was no argument from the volunteers as they walked through the camp. Nick could feel the peaceful emotions of those asleep and the anxiety of those still awake. They passed by a fire pit with an elderly man sitting and watching the flames, a haunted look in his eye. The man cast a glare in their direction and Nick could sense his distrust. The terror these people had gone through, being cast from their homes, in the name of a war that they had no say in, had taken a harsh toll. Nick met the man's gaze for a moment, trying to relay that he was not a threat, only here to help. Ajani led them into a large green canvas tent with cots lining the walls. The tent was lit with a single lantern hanging from the structural pole at the center. Lined up in the back were bins of medical equipment and supplies left by previous medical teams.

"During the night you sleep here and during the day we move the cots to set up medical stations and whatever else you need," Ajani said. The volunteers mumbled their thanks, and each found a cot to sleep on. They stashed their bags under their cots and added any medical supplies they'd brought to the pile along the back wall. All the volunteers worked quietly and quickly, eager for sleep. The couple that had ridden in the truck's cab with Ajani pushed two cots together and held hands as they whispered to each other for a few moments before attempting to sleep. The volunteer that had battled motion sickness for the past few hours was the first to drift off with a rhythmic snore.

Nick felt fatigued, but didn't feel the need to sleep. While lying down, he gazed at the top of the tent, absorbing the sounds both inside and outside. He tried to familiarize himself with the various sounds so that when he wished to sleep, they could fade into the background. Pondering over the book in his bag, he acknowledged that reading would be impossible in the tent because of the poor lighting. He couldn't read the words, anyway. He needed to focus on the task at hand. In the morning, their medical work would begin.

CHAPTER 12

Nick meditated through the night, dozing occasionally but not dreaming. The feeling of the camp was a mix of discouragement, fear, and helplessness. Despite the terrible situation in which these people had found themselves, he also felt a vein of hope running through the camp. That was part of the reason the medical teams came, to fuel that hope. Nick had expected these emotions. What surprised him was the nagging feeling that something was off, as if there was an unsettled darkness permeating in and around the other emotions. He wondered if it was because of the council room events a few days before. Nick pushed aside the negativity, knowing how easy it was to spiral, determined to stay vigilant.

The volunteers stirred as the first rays of sunshine filtered through the top of the tent, casting a greenish glow on all its tenants. Dust swirled in the light rays peeking through the small slits worn at the top of the tent. Nick stood and left the tent to find a place to relieve himself, but he stopped at the tent door. An elderly man with a bandaged leg used a makeshift crutch, while a woman held a sleeping child and a young boy coughed incessantly in line. Nick recognized the man with the crutch as the glaring man sitting by the fire the night before. The line continued around the edge of the tent and out of sight. Nick had heard there were around one hundred people in the displacement camp. At least half of them were standing in line for medical help.

"They will be with you soon," Nick promised to the injured man at the front of the line. He didn't know if he spoke English, but the man nodded as if he understood. Nick walked back into the tent and almost ran into the married man that rode in the truck's cab yesterday. His hair was tousled, but his eyes were bright. Nick gathered that this man, who had experience in this kind of mission, was the leader of the group.

"There is a line," he said to Nick, more a statement than a question. Nick nodded. "Alright team, let's get moving. Our organizer said it has been weeks since a medical team was here at camp. It's time to get to work." He began directing individual team members about where to set up and who would run each station. "I'm Jelani, by the way." The man paused his directing and reached out a hand. Nick returned his firm handshake.

"I'm Nick. I'll be right back to help however I can." Jelani barely acknowledged his response as he was called to help another volunteer sort through the available medical supplies. Nick slipped out the tent door into the beautiful, fresh morning air. As the sun rose, he was grateful for the moderate temperatures of this region, especially in these winter months. He walked around the edge of the camp before finding the squat latrine. The smell of urine and feces was strong, but he knew it was better than trying to find a private place somewhere out in the desert landscape.

Nick could hear the pots and pans clink together as breakfast preparations began around fire pits. He noticed the women working together and visiting, occasionally going from one fire to another to greet a friend. Children ran between fires, and it was impossible to tell which ones belonged to which women. The women treated all the children as if they were their own, calling them away from their play to bring more firewood or stir a pot while they went into the tent for a moment. The dangers of war had created this village and bonded the people. They relied on each other to survive.

In the short time Nick had been gone, the volunteers had set up two medical stations with more underway. The first station, just inside the tent doors, had the man with the bandaged leg, and Nick smelled the decay when he passed. Nick approached Jelani, who held a clipboard, taking inventory.

"How can I help?" Nick asked.

"Do you have medical training?"

"I've had years of experience caring for the sick and wounded."

"Oh, like hospice work?" Jelani didn't wait for a response. "Excellent, I'll have you help my wife, Asha, at station three." He led the way over to Asha.

"This is Nick..." Jelani looked at him, eyebrow raised for confirmation.

"Yes, that's me," he said, reaching out a hand to shake Asha's. "Just point me in a direction and I'll do whatever I can to help."

"Wonderful. It's great to meet you. Is this your first medical mission?" They talked back and forth about various missions they each served in and then got to work when Jelani ushered a patient to their station.

Nick spent the rest of the morning helping Asha with everything from holding children's arms while she disinfected a wound, to holding a flashlight, to refilling water bottles. He loved the hands-on service and loved the gratitude and cheerfulness of the people despite their hardships.

Asha herself was a force to be reckoned with. She moved quickly and seemed to never tire. With each energetic turn, she would push her long braid over her shoulder. She spoke kindly with each patient, helping them feel at ease. The medical team got through the line of refugees by late afternoon. Asha and Nick were the only ones left in the tent; they were sterilizing their station after helping an older woman with a sore on her leg when Nick felt a wave of nervousness. Asha had shown nothing but confidence that day. Where was this coming from? He glanced around the tent and saw a woman holding a toddler peeking nervously into the tent. Nick tapped Asha's arm and pointed toward the tent door. Asha went immediately to the tent door and greeted her. They spoke in hushed tones as Nick stored the leftover bandages in their tote.

"Nick, would you come here for a moment?" Asha called from the tent entrance. Asha surprised Nick by taking the toddler from the woman and handing him to Nick. "Would you mind taking little Kellen for a walk? Let me have a quick chat with his mama?" Nick didn't hesitate.

"Of course. Come on, little one! We'll be back in... twenty minutes?"

"That should be perfect," Asha said, untying the rope holding the tent door open then pushing it aside so he and Kellen could exit the tent. Nick set Kellen down. He reached a hand down to the boy as the tent door closed behind them. Kellen instinctively took Nick's offered hand.

"Well, what should we do?" Nick looked down at Kellen, who was most likely somewhere between two and three. Kellen let go of Nick's hand and walked down the row of tents. "Ok," Nick said to himself, with a small smile, "you lead the way." Nick followed Kellen as he walked through the center of the camp. He stopped him from getting too close to a fire pit twice, picked him up and set him down facing a different direction when he tried to enter one of the tents, and helped him find a smaller rock when the one he was trying to pick up was way too big for his little arms to carry. Kellen carried the small rock as they continued their wanderings around the camp as if it was a grand prize. Suddenly, Kellen broke into a run, moving between two tents, and out of Nick's sight. Nick walked quickly to catch up. He found the boy squatting down, looking closely at something that Nick couldn't quite see. Had he found another interesting rock? As Nick approached, he saw that the rock was oddly shaped and had specks of dark brown and yellow on it. Wait a second...

"Kellen, you found a frog!" Nick said in a complimentary tone. Kellen seemed pleased with his find and put his pointer finger out to poke the animal. Nick's reflexes were almost fast enough to save the creature. Almost. The boy's finger hit the frog right in the middle of its back. It let out a high-pitched squeak and took a few tiny steps backward. It continued its war cry for another few squeaks as Kellen giggled and went on all fours to get a closer look. If the frog didn't like being poked, it definitely didn't enjoy having a toddler's face so close to its own. It turned and scuttled off at a surprising speed. Nick scooped Kellen up so he wouldn't keep following the poor creature. Ben could have identified the creature by its scientific genome, listed what it ate, and when it was first discovered, but Nick was content with watching Kellen's joy in experiencing the interesting little creature. Nick went to move Kellen to his other hip and accidentally brushed the boy's foot with his hand. Kellen gave a sharp inhale and squirmed. Nick readjusted him and saw a small smear of blood on the back of his own hand. Nick quickly, but gently, grabbed Kellen's foot to see where the blood was coming from. On the boy's heel was a half-inch cut, lightly bleeding. It looked as if the skin had become dry and cracked.

"I believe it's time for us to return to the medical tent. What do you think? Should we go see mama?" Kellen perked up at the last word and Nick felt his excitement. He glanced at his watch to confirm that they'd been gone long enough and then headed back to the tent. The tent door was once again pulled open when they returned and so Nick felt confident they could enter. Kellen wiggled to get down as soon as he saw his mama, but Nick adjusted and held tight.

"We may have incurred a minor injury on our walk," Nick admitted, dropping the toddler into his mother's lap.

Asha cooed and fussed over the child, disinfecting and bandaging his foot while Kellen's mother sat next to him on the cot. Asha was simply glowing. Nick had a suspicion, so he focused his emotional powers on Asha. Nick could feel her love and compassion for the child and the joy she felt at interacting with him, but there was something else. A small emotion coming from deep inside her. An immature emotion, so new, and perfect, mostly instinct, but still individual. The feeling was of complete contentment and peace. A baby growing inside a mother's womb. Nick looked at Asha's smile and wondered if anyone else knew.

"Nick, my friend!" Ajani called from the opening of the tent with a wave. "Might I steal you away?" Nick looked at Asha. She didn't look up from her game of peekaboo with Kellen.

"I believe I have finished my work here for the day," he replied. "What can I do for you?"

Ajani led Nick to the back corner of the tent, where the extra cots were lined up.

"When we last communicated you mentioned bringing shoes?"

"Yes!" Stepping around Ajani, Nick retrieved his black bag from the spot where his cot had been pushed against the tent wall. "I have them here."

"May I accompany you to distribute them? Most people are out of their tents preparing their evening meal now. I wish to see their joy."

"Of course." Nick pulled an item out of his bag and placed it on top of his cot before closing the bag and throwing it over his shoulder.

"Did I hear you mention shoes?" Asha asked as they passed her station.

"Yes!" Ajani answered, "Our friend has brought shoes for everyone."

"Can we start with this little one?" Asha asked, gesturing to the toddler that was once again in his mother's arms. His cut will heal faster if he doesn't walk everywhere on his bandage." Nick dropped the bag to the ground. He pulled a few small pairs of shoes from the bag and beckoned the mother over.

"For him?" she asked when seeing the contents of the bag, pointing to her son.

"And you as well," Nick said, gesturing to her bare feet. The mother grabbed Nick's hands.

"Thank you," she whispered, squeezing his hands. She helped him sort through and found a pair that would fit her son. Nick gave her a pair that were the next size up as well, knowing how fast little feet grow. They said goodbye to the women and headed toward the tent closest to the medical tent. They had conquered the line, but Nick was sure they'd have more patients trickling in the entire time they were here.

A group of women worked around a fire pit in front of their neighboring tent. One woman leaned over a pan while the other mixed dough in a bowl. Nick approached, and Ajani greeted them in their language. He explained that Nick had brought shoes and their faces brightened. He dropped his bag to the ground and the woman with the bowl called into the tent. Nick's bag was soon surrounded. An elderly woman and two children shuffled through, trying on different shoes until they each found an acceptable fit. The elderly woman reached for Nick's face. She patted his cheek and he felt the aged wisdom and warmth coming from her. This scene repeated as they attended each tent in the camp. Nick and Ajani returned to the medical tent with only a dozen pairs left.

Ajani showed him a bin where he could leave the shoes for later. The backup shoes would come in useful as children's feet grew and old shoes continued to wear out.

"Hey there!" Nick heard from behind him. He turned to see the talkative woman with the red hair standing right behind him.

"Hello," Nick said, grimacing at his own formality. Sometimes he wondered if his generations on this earth showed in his language.

"I'm Sariah. I tried to introduce myself on the truck yesterday, but it was so loud!" She chuckled at the memory. "This is my first medical mission, so I wasn't sure what to expect and boy was that a wild ride. And today has been a whirlwind. I'm so glad I could be here to help. My roommates back at the school think I'm crazy for coming to this part of the country with all the wars and cartels and everything, but I just want to help. It's why I am getting my medical degree. I was so blessed to grow up with two working parents and a pleasant home. I just want to help those that didn't get as lucky. Are you a medical student? Oh, wait, no, Asha said you were just helping. That's right. What brings you out this way? You don't look like a local, if you don't mind me saying."

Nick's eyes widened, impressed by Sariah's enthusiasm and ability to say so many words in one breath.

"I'm Nick. No, not a medical student, just here to help in any way I can. I admire your tenacity and passion for service."

"Thanks." Sariah beamed. "I get it from my mom. She was always helping others. Taking meals to the sick, volunteering at the schools I attended, and dropping everything to help a neighbor." Her eyes glazed over as she reminisced about the service from her mother.

"A wonderful woman," Nick said. "I'm so glad you had the support that led you here. Family fulfills an essential role in raising the next generation."

"It does, and it's great to meet you. I'd better finish packing away my station so we can get cots out for the night. Sounds like vaccines are on the schedule for tomorrow, then lots of follow up work for the next few weeks." Sariah's eyes sparkled at the thought.

"Do you need help with putting away your station?"

"I think you'd be better off finding a good use for that." Sariah gestured to the last thing Nick had pulled from his bag.

"I'm sure you're right," he said with a twinkle in his eye. "If you ever need anything, please ask. It's why I'm here." That and the promptings from the Creator, he thought. As Sariah walked away, he thought about how she could probably give Jack a run for his money. Maybe even keep up with his quick wit and energy. Nick grabbed the last item, tucked it under his arm, and headed out into the camp.

CHAPTER 13

Nick didn't have to go far. At the first tent he walked past, a young boy ran up to him. He called over his shoulder to a friend or sibling, Nick wasn't sure which. Both boys gathered around and Nick knelt down to their eye level.

"You boys know what this is?" he asked, hoping they could understand. He pulled the black and white ball out from underneath his arm and held it toward the boys.

"Football!" they exclaimed together.

"Is your work done? Have you been helpful today?"

"Yes, sir," the boys said, nodding enthusiastically. He looked at the women watching from their fire pit. The closest one, possibly the mother, pretended to debate and then gave a small nod.

"Well, then, this is for you." The boys were in awe and seemed hesitant to take the ball. Nick placed it in one of the boy's hands.

"Let's go see who else is done with their work for the day!" Nick said. The boy raised the ball above his head and ran, holding it in the air chanting, "football, football!" and that was all it took for a group of children to gather. Nick watched as they stood in a circle and kicked the ball back and forth. After a while, they split into two teams and started playing a version of the game the ball was meant for, but in the end, it could only be described as chaos. The children didn't care about the rules or goals. They just wanted a chance to kick the ball. The smiles and laughter of the children, getting to watch them be kids in such a hard situation, made all the difficulties of getting to the refugee camp worth it. These were the moments that helped balance out everything else. The ball rolled to Nick's feet and all the children paused, looking to see what he would do. He looked up, raised an eyebrow, and then kicked the ball up into the air with the toe of his boot. He caught it on his foot, kicked it up and bounced it on his knee a few times. Then he kicked it at a small girl at the edge of the group. She looked at the ball, uncertainty clouding her eyes, and then she smiled and kicked it back to the center of all the kids. They laughed and continued playing until darkness settled over the desert and adults called children to their tents.

Returning to the volunteer tent, Nick saw through the opened door that someone had returned all the cots to where they were last night. A few of the medical volunteers were making a kind of meatless stew over the firepit in front of the tent.

"You are their hero," a volunteer said to Nick as he came around the fire.

"Oh, no, they are the heroes. The children have no say in the war. They are the most innocent and get dragged through everything. They have to grow up so quickly. I'm happy to provide some joy and distraction amidst it all," Nick said sincerely. Ajani joined them around the fire just as a volunteer handed out tin cups full of the soup.

"Good work today, so much good. Thank you. The shoes, the medicine. It is so important." Ajani's voice carried deep emotion.

Nick learned the names of the other volunteers as they ate their late dinner. They exchanged notes on different patients they'd seen that day, inquired after various medical equipment available, and talked about where they were all from. Nick was content to listen and give vague responses when asked a direct question. The conversation moved on so quickly that no one seemed to notice. When dinner was over, they all returned to their cots satisfied with the day's work and prepared for more ahead.

CHAPTER 14

The days continued much the same – awake with the sun, help the medical students, and then 'football' with the children. The medical team helped with every case they could. Occasionally, they would find someone who needed more help than they could provide at the camp. These were the saddest cases. Access to a hospital and full medical care could ease a lot of suffering.

Nick became familiar with the faces in camp and learned a lot of names. Sometimes a kid would wander into the medical tent to find him, throwing their arms around him, and asking endless questions before a parent or sibling found them and made them return to their chores.

"The children love you," Sariah observed after watching yet another child being redirected out of the tent. They washed their hands at the makeshift sink and headed out of the tent to get lunch.

"Children have a great capacity for love," was Nick's response.

"And trouble." Sariah laughed. "I have three little brothers and oh, the grief they gave my parents when they were younger. Actually, they still do, even with only one of them still at home."

"I'm sure they do," Nick said.

"Do you have siblings?" Sariah asked. These were the kinds of questions Nick tried to avoid. He grabbed a packaged sandwich from the box of food Ajani had brought from a trip to the city earlier in the week.

"I don't."

"An only child! I always wondered what that would be like." Sariah continued in her fast-paced monologue about only children that then turned to her questioning what she would have even done without her brothers. Nick listened, nodding occasionally. Conversations with Sariah required little effort on his end, and he just let her continue, not feeling the need to correct her misunderstanding. It isn't easy to explain why he didn't have siblings, or parents, at least not in the traditional sense.

"Can you believe we've been here a month already? Christmas came and went like that." She snapped her fingers. "A couple of babies are due soon. I bet we'll be here to help deliver them." Nick looked at his watch, as if that would help him wrap his mind around the time that had passed.

"That's amazing. Halfway through our time here," Nick squeezed in before Sariah continued.

"I think it's because we've been so busy. Those first few days were such a blur, but now that we've settled into a comfortable routine and are getting to know the people, it is still flying by. Have you met Salana? What a character, and he has the backstory to match! I think he would talk to you all day if you had the time." Nick smiled internally at this verbose description of a fellow loquacious individual. He'd had a few conversations with Salana since seeing him glare in their direction when they first arrived, and he agreed with Sariah's assessment.

Nick continued to listen as he ate his sandwich and bag of popcorn. He dismissed himself to go look for a piece of fruit. He found a very brown banana, but not knowing when the next chance for fresh fruit would be, he peeled and ate the very soft, bruised banana. His eyes fell on Asha, who motioned for him to sit beside her and Jelani. Asha's stomach showed signs of her condition. As far as he knew, no one else had noticed, but Nick knew her secret and that made the signs obvious. He kept catching Jelani looking at his wife with eyes full of love and concern. Nick believed they hadn't mentioned it because this area of the world often discouraged pregnant women from participating in medical missions. They would face exposure to many diseases and infections, and there were very limited options for prenatal care.

A feeling of alarm overtook Nick. He stood abruptly. Sariah stopped talking and everyone around the fire turned to look at him, but not for long. All attention shifted to a man running up to the fire where the volunteers sat or stood eating. The runner clutched his hand to his chest, his breath coming in wheezes.

"Ajani?" he choked out between his chest caving inhales. Sariah pointed toward the tent where Ajani was resting. The camp came alive with activity and alarm. Something was happening and Nick could feel the fear. Ajani emerged from the tent seconds later, discussing with the runner in a low voice. Their conversation ended and with a nod to Ajani and then the volunteers, before the man sprinted off again. The volunteers all sat stunned, some with forkfuls of food halfway to their mouths.

"Kofi says there is a jeep approaching the camp quickly from the east." Everyone understood the seriousness of the situation. The refugees had fled from the East. Warlords and violence had pushed them further and further west. Now it seemed they were coming to find them again. "It will be here in a matter of minutes. Everyone must go into their tents and stay as quiet as possible. We don't want to seem like a threat. Do not come out until someone comes for you. I will go meet the driver as far from camp as possible," Ajani said quickly. In his hand he held a white cloth. A silence fell among the volunteers and then everyone moved at once. They left their food where it was and retreated to the tent.

"Ajani, let me come with you," Nick asked once all the other volunteers were in the tent.

"No, it is too dangerous. If they see a white man, they may become more violent. They do not trust."

"I understand." Nick nodded and headed into the tent. He heard Ajani's footsteps fade and could feel him buoying himself up. Nick felt Ajani's courage amidst his fear. Nick paced the back of the tent, rubbing at his beard. The other volunteers sat on their cots, waiting. Some sat on the same cots, comforting one another, and whispering stories of this happening on other missions they'd been on. Nick felt he'd waited long enough. He headed toward the tent door.

"You must stay. It isn't safe for any of us if you are seen," Asha said from the cot where she sat with her husband, his arm wrapped protectively across her shoulders.

"I will stay out of sight." He didn't give them any more time to protest. He pushed aside the canvas door and hurried behind the tent. In the middle of the day, with the sun directly overhead and scarce shade available, he traversed the camp by staying in the shadows of the tents. Whispering from inside tents caused his ears to tense as he passed, but louder voices on the eastern side of the camp drew his attention.

"These people are no threat. We have nothing. There are sick among us, women about to give birth. We can't just leave." Nick heard Ajani's plea over the sound of the idling jeep as he came to the edge of the last tent in the camp. He peered around the edge of the canvas and saw Ajani holding his white cloth. It waved in his hand with each panicked statement. A man with camouflage pants and a white sleeveless shirt stood facing Ajani. His exposed arms and chest glistened in the heat. Nick recognized the brand burned into the top of the man's arm. He was a cartel leader, one of many responsible for wars raging in this country. The man had a mark where the strap of his gun had chaffed across the skin of his neck. Two large men stood as guards on either side of the man. They wore the same camouflage pants, black shirts, and deep scowls. They held their arms crossed in front of them, their guns slung across their backs.

"I have come as a courtesy. The next time there will be many more men, and many more guns," the man said before raising his voice as if calling to the entire camp, "You must leave or die." Ajani opened his mouth to protest more, but the cartel leader shot his weapon into the air, silencing him. People within the camp let out muffled screams and cries. The leader turned, giving commands to his two guards, and they followed him back to their jeep.

Nick had heard enough. He walked back to the medical tent, his mind reeling.

CHAPTER 15

The panic and anxiety that filled the refugees sapped energy from Nick. Others could sense it, too. It was like a fog filling in the space between everyone and their movement. There was weariness in the eyes of the adults and confusion in the eyes of the children. Ajani had everyone gathered outside of the medical tent. Everyone was on their feet, shifting nervously, waiting for direction.

"We've been warned and we're going to take it seriously," Ajani called out to the crowd. "We will not wait for more men with more guns to come. At the break of dawn, we will begin packing and start our journey."

"Where will we go?" a voice called from the gathered refugees.

"Further west. I need to return the medical team to Johannesburg. They cannot stay under this threat. Kofi," he nodded toward the runner from earlier, "will lead the breaking of camp and the start of the journey. We will travel in groups. I will reach out to my contacts about resettlement, but I fear the men will return before we can make arrangements. It's up to us to move to safety. I will return as quickly as I can," Ajani said.

"I will stay." Nick raised his arm. "I will help with resettlement. We may need to retreat as far as the mountains." Ajani did not doubt Nick's sincerity.

"Kofi, work together with Nick," Ajani directed, then turned to address the gathering again. "Everyone, go back to your tents and sort through what must come, and what can be left behind. Ajani instructed. "I will leave at first light. We must begin as soon as we can and be on our way before the men return."

"When will they return?" Nick asked.

"They didn't say. Which makes it that much more urgent." Nick thought about their long journey to camp in Ajani's beat up truck. It would take days to reach the mountains by foot.

Everyone paused as if hoping for more instruction, then realizing there would be none, slowly walked back to their own tents, whispering urgently to each other. As the crowd dispersed, a woman remained behind, her pregnant belly protruding underneath her worn dress. She approached Ajani, her shoes leaving dusty footprints with each step.

"I cannot make this journey. My baby is coming. You are sending away the doctors..." Her voice trailed off as her eyes filled with tears. Ajani's eyes reflected the woman's concern, and he took one of her hands in his own.

"Do you have family in the camp?" he asked.

"Only my grandmother, who will also struggle with the journey." She paused, looking around at the retreating refugees. "I suppose there is no choice?" Her eyes pleaded for another solution.

"I am sorry. There is not. We must move. Let others pack the essentials and take down tents. Reserve your energy for walking. Find an experienced mother among our camp that can feel confident in delivering a baby along the way if needed," Ajani instructed. A tear fell down the mother-to-be's eyes.

"And if the baby comes? I am already having pains each night," she said, her voice choked.

"Let it be God's will," Ajani said reverently. Nick stepped forward, extending his arm.

"May I walk you back to your tent?" The sun was beginning its descent and there was much to do. The woman's eyes looked between Nick and Ajani before she accepted his offered arm. He realized this was an antiquated gentlemanly move, but some habits are hard to break. He didn't miss cravats or stifling high collared shirts, but sometimes he missed the simple respectful gestures like escorting women or standing when they entered a room. Since the global pandemic, even a basic handshake was rare.

"Nick?" the woman asked.

"You know my name?" he asked, surprised.

"You are all the children talk about. The white man that brought the football," she laughed, placing her free hand around her belly. "I am Lidiya."

"It is a pleasure to officially meet you. I believe I've seen you around."

"I'm hard to miss!" Lidiya said, with another small laugh. Her shoulders fell as her laughter faded. Nick could feel the fear returning.

"Nick?" Lidiya said again, "Why do you stay? You could be safe with the medical team. You could go home." Nick took a moment to compose his answer.

"It really never occurred to me to leave. I prefer to be where help is needed. I've been among all of you for weeks now. Many of you have become friends. Who am I to leave when things get hard? My life is no more important than any of yours." The woman paused to catch her breath, though they hadn't gone far. She cringed and tried to stand straighter. Nick felt the woman's discomfort and fear, but deep within her, he felt nothing but love and peace. The baby knew nothing of this world or its mother's challenges. Nick placed a hand on top of Lidiya's hand on his arm and transferred a word that they were all going to need in the coming days and weeks. *Courage.*

Lidiya resumed their slow pace, her breathing returning to normal. Nick could feel the shift as the word and emotions bounced around within her, looking for a place to latch onto and spread. By the time they had reached Lidiya's tent, Nick knew the courage had taken root. She dropped her hand from his arm and walked toward her tent. She would be a force for good, an inspiration to the others in camp.

As Lidiya approached, three women emerged from the tent. "Lidiya, we worried. Where were you?" an older woman asked sternly. Nick assumed it was her grandmother.

"Just discussing matters with Ajani and Nick." Lidiya waved in Nick's direction.

"Come in and rest," a younger woman said, putting her arm around Lidiya's waist and walking her into the tent. The older woman called Nick's name, stopping him from leaving.

"Thank you for walking her back. This is her first baby, and she has been so worried, as she should be." She lowered her voice and stepped closer to Nick. "Her husband was killed not long before we stumbled into this camp. She was so thin and frail. The poor babe was taking all her energy. She could not eat or drink. I was so scared for her."

"You ladies have done a wonderful job of nursing her back to health," Nick said. The aged woman smiled.

"We are doing our best to take care of each other. We are all some of us have. Have a blessed night, Nick." He gave a slight bow and continued back to the medical tent.

CHAPTER 16

Asha was in a whispered argument with her husband amidst the chaos of the scrambling volunteers. Nick tried not to overhear as he began packing the equipment at the station next to theirs, but it was difficult as their whispers became louder.

"We must stay and help," Asha pleaded. "There are babies about to be born, infections still being treated. We can't just abandon them."

"You know the rules. When there is a direct threat to the safety of the refugees or volunteers, we have to return," Jelani said, still packing things into a tote with a red medical sign on the front.

"Nick asked to stay. We could too." Asha planted her feet firmly beside her husband, arms crossed, brows furrowed.

"Asha," Jelani said softly, "it was already a risk coming in your condition, but you insisted. If Ajani or anyone else knew, they would feel the same way I do. We must get you home." He glanced around to make sure they were not being overheard. Asha sniffed, wiping a hand beneath her nose. She kept her firm stance facing her husband but looked pointedly away, her jaw clenched.

"Fine," she finally said, "but I'm not happy about it. I will always wonder if everyone is okay or if my staying could have made a difference." Jelani secured the lid on the tote and turned to her.

"I know, my love, I know. Your heart is pure gold and if we're lucky, our child will be just like *her* mama."

"Or *his* papa," she whispered, wrapping her arms around her husband.

Nick felt he had intruded on a private moment as he continued packing away medical equipment, but his heart soared at the goodness of the couple. Their willingness to sacrifice for strangers and then ultimately sacrifice for the wellbeing of their child was honorable. Amidst such dark and daunting circumstances, they were a light.

Before laying on his cot for possibly the last time, he pulled the ancient book from his bag and sat with his back to the rest of the volunteers. Glancing behind him, he saw that everyone was either attempting sleep or otherwise occupied. He flipped through the pages until he came to the torn page. He ran a finger carefully along the tear while his mind tried to wrap around the meaning of the events leading up to his time in Ethiopia. He gently placed the book back into his bag and laid down, looking up at the canvas of the tent. He pushed away the anxious energy of the camp and reached for the Creator in his mind. He felt the normal peace that came during these times of meditation. He felt his worries about taking the book eased, and tried to let sleep overtake him, knowing that the morning would be taxing for everyone.

***

The next morning the medical volunteers loaded into the back of Ajani's truck, and left. Sariah had wrapped her arms around Nick and given him a tight squeeze. Another volunteer had to take Sariah's arm and lead her to the truck as she babbled on about precautions Nick needed to take and which of her patients needed follow up care.

If it weren't for the roaring of the engine of Ajani's truck, they would've slipped away unnoticed. A frantic energy filled the camp. Pots and pans clanged. Every tent echoed with discussions and arguments about what qualified as essential and who would carry what. They took down the tents and piled them together. They wouldn't be able to carry those. Ajani would have to return with the truck, or perhaps they would simply have to abandon them for the cartel to pilfer.

Kofi created groups for traveling, which included a combination of the elderly, sick, and able-bodied. He would lead out with the first group. Nick would oversee the completion of breaking down the camp and leave with the last group. The groups would move out one after the other, staying close, but putting some space between groups so they didn't form one giant pack trying to walk a narrow trail.

They placed Lydia in his group along with her grandmother and a confident woman who believed she could help deliver a baby if needed. They'd been referring to the woman as 'the midwife', and she stopped protesting after the first few times. Oh, how Nick hoped they wouldn't have to deliver a possibly premature baby on the journey. He'd done a lot of intense and uncomfortable things in all his years on the earth, but delivering a baby had not been one of them. There were a few other women in the group as well, each with a few children of their own. The men had all opted to go ahead in order to set up the new camp when they reached a safe destination. Nick stood facing his small group.

"Are we all ready? Is there anything we've forgotten? Is everyone confident in what they are carrying? Don't be afraid to ask for help or to change packs with another person for a while. Together, we're going to do this." Lidiya's grandmother gave Lidiya's elbow a squeeze, and they exchanged small smiles. They all turned to walk the path they'd watched all the other groups disappear on when a child in the group pulled at Nick's arm.

"Yes?" he asked, eyebrows raised. The boy only pointed behind them. A plume of dirt rose in the distance. Nick's heart dropped. He looked ahead of them and squinted to see the line of refugees walking toward safer territory. With a firm grip on the boy's hand, he walked him a few quick steps to Lidiya. He placed the boy's hand in hers. She looked at the boy and then at Nick, confused. He gave a reassuring smile, and she squeezed the boy's hand.

"Stay with her, help her around rocks and sharp plants. Can you do that for me?" Nick asked. The boy nodded and stood taller. He took Nick's request seriously and fell into step alongside Lidiya. He hoped Lidiya understood it was as much for the boy's safety as it was for her benefit.

"No matter what happens, keep walking," Nick said sternly. Lidiya nodded, her eyes reflecting the courage she had accepted last night.

Nick turned around and ran toward the quickly approaching vehicle, hoping it would stop far away from the retreating refugees.

CHAPTER 17

The black jeep rumbled to a stop ten feet in front of Nick. He glanced over his shoulder. In the few minutes he'd waited for the jeep, his group had made good progress and were well on their way. He could make out the distinct sway and arch of Lidiya and the boy helping her with each step. Her grandmother was close to her on the other side. They moved as quickly as possible with the new approaching threat.

Nick turned back and waited patiently for the men to approach. His heart pounded in his chest as he sent a plea to the Creator for a quick resolution and safety for the refugees. He eyed the guns warily as the men approached. He knew he couldn't die. There had been many opportunities for that through the years, but he did know pain. He knew the deep bruising of a bullet hitting him, thanks to previous wars he fought in. The protectors might heal faster than mortals, but they could feel pain just the same. Nick recognized the man in the middle as the same one Ajani pleaded with the night before. The two men with him were at least a head taller than their boss.

"Who are you..." The leader let out a string of racial slurs. Nick pretended not to hear. He didn't give an answer, and a guard approached him.

"Answer him," the guard said, pushing Nick's chest with his gun. Nick stumbled, but remained silent. The man grabbed Nick's arm and jerked it around and behind his back. He grabbed the other arm and roughly tied Nick's hands together at the wrist. Nick didn't resist. The longer these men kept their focus on him, the further away the refugees could flee. The ropes tying him weren't overly tight, which he was grateful for. Nick was no threat to these men, and he sensed that they knew it.

"Don't be stupid," the guard snarled at Nick, pushing him down to his knees, keeping one hand pressed into his shoulder.

"The people have left, so you have no business here. Everyone has done as you asked," Nick said, breaking his silence. The branded cartel leader looked around at the abandoned supplies. He nudged some tents with his toe. He turned to his other guard and spoke quickly in a language that Nick couldn't understand. The guard began hauling tents into the back of their truck. Nick's stomach twisted at the thieving.

"We take what we want," the man said, to no one in particular. He had yet to look Nick in the eye. Nick watched wordlessly, as the two men loaded as many tents and supplies into their jeep as they could. He was relieved to see a few medical totes and two tents left behind. That would at least give them something to work with as they resettled. They tightened a tarp over the load, the weight of their haul causing the back of the jeep to sit low on its tires. The leader gave another sharp instruction to his guard. The guard walked to the remaining supplies and began flicking a lighter to life. Nick's heart rate increased.

"No!" he shouted. The words came before he could stop himself. The leader ran to Nick, lifted his gun, and swung it toward his head. Nick's instincts kicked in and he ducked down, feeling the rush of the gun above his head. He kicked out his right leg, spinning on his left knee, and kicked the leader's legs out from under him. He fell with an angry grunt.

The consequences were instant. The guard behind him pulled him to his feet, and plunged his fist right into his stomach. Nick doubled over and fell back to his knees. The leader got back to his feet and grabbed Nick's hair, pulling back to expose his neck. He hated this position.

"I should kill you," he hissed. He pulled a knife from his pocket and pressed it to Nick's neck. He could feel a sharp sting and trickle of blood run from where it pressed into him. Nick smelled burning plastic and looked from the corner of his eyes to see black smoldering smoke coming from the corner of the supplies. His anger flared and he wrestled with his urge to fight. He held as still as he could, feeling the cartel leader's rage settle to contempt.

The leader slowly removed the knife and stood. He turned his back and then, as if changing his mind, turned and kicked him in the back with all his strength. Nick' back arched and then he curled into himself bracing for the next blow. A boot crashed into the side of his head and he saw lights behind his closed eyes. A mortal would have been knocked out, or worse. Nick remained perfectly still aside from his shallow breathing.

"Leave him," the cartel leader said, spitting at Nick. The spittle landed an inch from his face. "We'll let the elements end him. Maybe a wild beast will pull the flesh from his bones before he dies of dehydration." The two guards laughed as they returned to the jeep. As quickly as they came, they left, leaving Nick lying on the ground on his side, rocks and dirt pressed into his bare forearm, his hands bound behind his back. The sound of the jeep faded, and another sound caught Nick's attention - the fire.

Nick pushed against his shoulder and used his elbow to get into a kneeling position. The guard that lit the fire hadn't tried too hard, and the fire was still small, smoldering on a plastic tarp. He pushed to his feet, pausing for a heartbeat as the blood rushed in his ears, then kicked dirt onto the fire. Once it was reduced to a few small flames, Nick stamped it out with his boot. The fire rendered a tent useless and melted a corner of a medical bin, but the rest of the supplies remained intact and hopefully Ajani could pick them up on his return.

Nick felt relieved that the threat had passed, but then his stomach tightened at the thought of the journey these people had in front of them. He walked to where he'd dropped his staff and kicked it up to lean against him. It took several attempts, but he was able to get the staff into the rope around his hands and use it as a lever to create more space and slid his hands free. Rubbing his wrists, he squinted to where his group had disappeared into the distance. He couldn't see them, but knew where they'd gone. He attempted a deep breath, but stopped before fully filling his lungs. Bracing himself against his staff, he coughed out a laugh. His abdomen was going to be sore for a while. Pushing through the pain, he set a quick pace to catch up with his group.

CHAPTER 18
North Carolina 1862

Nick's knees hit the ground, his head pushed into the canvas of the tent as his hands were being tied behind his back. Their plan was working perfectly. He heard the thud of his fellow officers hitting the ground next to him. He held his breath and tried to decipher the emotions in the room. Fear can be an overpowering one and it was the prominent one in the men closest to him. The next strongest emotion in the tent was anger. He heard that familiar sound of a rifle being loaded.

"What do you want?" his comrade beside him asked, straining his neck to see the confederate attackers behind them. They ignored the officer's question as the chaos of the intrusion settled.

"Take this one. He looks like he'll talk," a deep commanding voice ordered. Nick could smell the sweat and alcohol on the men as they dragged him to his feet and pushed him into a wooden chair. The only chair in the tent, reserved for the Major General. With a quick glance, Nick spotted seven armed men in grey wool jackets and trousers, their attire standing out against the white canvas walls of the tent. The man barking instructions wore a general's uniform coat. Nick pulled his head back as a man leaned down and put his face so close to Nick's that he could feel the man's brown mustache against his nose. Nick thought this very foolish since he could easily throw his head forward and smash the man's face, but he wouldn't. He needed to give Kaida enough time to gather the maps.

Kaida had been working for months as a nurse among the confederate troops, waiting to hear the right information that would give them an advantage in this war. Finally, it had come. Kaida had forged the right paperwork and landed Nick in the perfect position, a colonel in the union army. A higher rank, giving him some sway, but not so high that his disappearance would be overly obvious. Now he needed to play his part well so she could do her part. Someone had proposed the Anaconda Plan. There was just one thing that they needed - a map of all the southern ports. They needed a more precise idea before bringing in their troops and dividing the confederate army. Nick and Kaida strategically positioned themselves so he could propose the idea of infiltrating southern territory where they knew the port maps were kept. Kaida got herself 'promoted' to head nurse, which gave her the chance to blend in and become the perfect spy.

The general grabbed Nick's hair, pulling back his head, exposing his neck. The vulnerability of the pose caused a spark of panic, but he was able to rein it in. He had a job to do. Again, the general was in Nick's face.

"Tell me..." He moved Nick's head to the side and looked at the bird on his shoulder strap. "Colonel, why are you here? Our intelligence tells us that union troops are further north and yet, here you are, with a tent, like you are planning to camp out along our shores. You know you are not welcome here. I want to know why." He released Nick's head and took a step back, expecting an answer.

"I guess your intelligence was wrong then, because here we are," Nick said, rolling his neck to counter the awkward position the confederate had held him in. He heard the hit before he felt the jarring in his jaw.

"Why are you here?" The general shouted. Nick remained silent. Another hit, this one across his temple.

"You'll break, they always do." He sneered and pulled his arm back. Before he could strike again, the man's attention turned to the small yelp of surprise at the entrance of the tent.

"Oh, I'm so sorry, I brought the... oh, never mind. I'll leave. This just... oh!" Kaida dropped her tray of bandages as she faked a hasty retreat. That was the signal. Kaida had the maps. The men that they'd stationed in the woods would hear the crash and be coming shortly. Nick could feel their rapid heartbeats and sense their apprehension.

The man walked to Kaida, where she was picking up bandages and placing them back on the tray. He grabbed her arm and gave her a shake, causing her to drop the bandages in her hand. He lifted her to her feet with one hand and shoved her out of the tent. Nick heard a muffled thump he believed was Kaida's many layers of skirts hitting the ground. He couldn't sense Kaida's anger, but he could definitely feel his own at seeing her treated like that. It had taken all his willpower and belief in their purpose to not call out when the general grabbed her. The general returned to Nick, grabbing a handful of dark blue wool. The man's force caused a brass button to fall from the front of Nick's coat.

"One last chance, Colonel. Why are..." The man released Nick's coat and stumbled back, the loud clang of a tray echoing into the night. Three young union officers soon surrounded the general, and a dozen more were rushing to the aid of his comrades. Kaida stood with the tray at her side. Nick smiled, seeing the satisfied look on her face. As their men detained and tied the Confederate soldiers, Kaida untied Nick.

"I take it you got the maps?" Nick asked, rubbing his wrist and moving to his feet.

"With these scoundrels out of the way, it was easy. I slipped in and out of their cabin unnoticed. If the Union moves quickly, they'll be able to begin the naval blockade without any suspicion," she answered, digging into her deep apron pockets. Nick could see her cloak, but everyone else most likely only saw a black cotton dress and a long white apron. People would easily recognize her as a nurse. Kaida pulled out a thick stack of rolled maps and placed them in Nick's hand.

"What is your plan now?" Nick asked Kaida.

"Ireland. There is a friend in the government who might take actions to prevent further famine if persuaded. I will NOT be working as a nurse," she said adamantly. "I just... am really not good with sick people." She shuddered as the two of them left the tent. Nick could see Kaida not having much patience for the minor aches and pains of others. "What about you?" she asked.

"I'm going to make sure these," Nick said, lifting the roll of maps, "land in the right hands and then take my leave. While this war is just beginning, I believe our efforts have helped tip the scale in a direction pleasing to the Creator. I'll see where else I am needed."

"Colonel!" a soldier called from inside the tent.

"You'd better go. I will see you at council," Kaida said, looking around strategically. She pulled the reins of a confederate horse off a tree branch and mounted. The horse hesitated for a moment at the unfamiliar rider but broke into a trot as soon as Kaida's boots pressed into its sides. Her golden cloak billowed behind her as she rode off and Nick watched until he could no longer see her horse fading into the darkness.

CHAPTER 19

Nick wasn't surprised that his mind remembered that day during the civil war, with the similar treatment he'd just received. His mind replayed a few other scenarios from the same time period as he listened to the repetitive sound of his own footsteps on the uneven ground. He had followed the footsteps leading west, knowing he'd run into his group, eventually. His pace was notably swifter than that of a pregnant or elderly woman. His head snapped up when he heard a loud groan from the distance. He looked up to find Lidiya and her grandmother sitting on the path. Nick ran to close the distance. The midwife was there as well. She stood and waved her hands frantically at Nick to stop him from approaching. Nick could understand the cultural need for there to be no men if Lidiya was giving birth, but he hoped she would be lenient under the circumstances. He definitely wasn't the first person you'd want to help deliver a baby, but he could still be helpful.

"No, it is alright," Lidiya said breathlessly. "He is safe." Nick approached cautiously and knelt next to her, taking her hand in his own.

"She is having regular pains, a few minutes apart. The fast pace has been too much," the midwife muttered to Nick.

"Where is the pain?" Nick asked Lidiya directly.

"It is here," she said, nodding to the arm wrapped low around her protruding belly. Her grandmother scooted closer to help support Lidiya's back. She let out a groan and pressed her hand to her lower back, arching against the discomfort. "And in my back. I feel it, the baby, she wants to come."

"Oh, it's a she now, is it?" Nick said, eyebrows raised, trying to lighten the mood. She only glared and squeezed his hand through a contraction. Nick focused on seeing past the mother's fear and pain. He had never tried this, but had to do something. This baby is coming too soon, and the conditions will be harsh enough when they arrive. He hoped everyone would be better prepared. He narrowed in on the baby's emotions. The distress was obvious, and the powerful kicks and tumbles were likely causing the early contractions. He dug deep within himself, placed a hand on Lidiya's arm, and sent the word *calm* deep inside her. He pulled a water bottle from his bag and tipped it back for Lidiya to drink. After she had her fill, he handed it to Lidiya's grandmother. She looked terrified and drained. She gladly accepted the water. Lidiya shifted, so that she leaned on both hands behind her. Sweat gathered on her brow. Nick and the midwife sat in silence, allowing Lidiya to breathe. Her eyes were closed. Her breaths that were sharp and panicked when Nick arrived had slowly steadied. She opened her eyes and looked at the two of them.

"It has stopped," she said, her eyes full of concern and wonder.

"You know what?" Nick said slyly. "I think you are right. You carry a very brave, strong little girl."

"So strong," Lidiya agreed. Nick removed his bag and placed it so Lidiya could lie down and rest her head on it. The four of them rested and waited for another half hour and once Lidiya convinced everyone the contractions had truly stopped, they began their journey again at an incredibly slow pace. Nick and the midwife insisted on frequent breaks, despite Lidiya's insistence that she felt fine.

"Oh Lidiya, they are just being kind. The stops are for me, not you," Lidiya's grandmother said. Lidiya never complained about taking a break after that.

As darkness fell, they moved to the side of the path, next to a large rock that could protect against any wind during the night. They all did their best to sleep, despite the hard ground and nefarious situation. Nick always had his ears trained for any hint of an approaching vehicle.

On the second day, the terrain became softer, sandier, making it harder with each step. Trees appeared every few yards, providing a brief respite from the blazing sun. They continued at a slow, steady pace, in this same pattern for three days before coming to the new camp. The camp had no tents, only blankets hung from the branches of dead trees. The women of the camp swarmed Lidiya as soon as they saw her- asking how she felt and how the journey went. Nick stepped away, knowing she was in expert hands.

"I am so relieved to see you. I thought for sure they would kill you," Kofi said. Nick was momentarily stunned by his bluntness.

"No, still here." He exhaled, hoping his exhaustion didn't show.

"The boy told me about your bravery in facing down the men. Ajani himself couldn't have done better. Thank you," Kofi continued, placing a hand on Nick's shoulder. They both looked around at the shabby camp, surrounded by sparse trees, most of which were dead.

"Has Ajani returned? Is there any word?" Nick asked.

"Not yet, but we must keep our hope," Nick again understood why Kofi was chosen. His optimism was contagious.

As night settled over the camp, Nick wandered to check on Lidiya. She had found a resting place on a blanket, surrounded by many of the women that came to her aid as soon as she approached camp. She sat up when she noticed Nick.

"I feel as though you saved us. My baby was going to come. I could feel it."

"You and your baby are incredibly strong. Rest. You will meet your little one soon," Nick said encouragingly.

"Then perhaps I will be able to sleep again." She laughed.

"One thing is certain," Nick said, glancing around. "You will have many helpers." A murmur of agreement went amongst the women surrounding Lidiya. The kinship these women had created for each other impressed Nick. It made no difference to them who was related by blood. They became each other's family.

Ajani returned two days later with the supplies they had left behind and a box of much needed food. It didn't spread far, but they made the most of it. His report of a supply truck coming soon lifted their spirits. Ajani's truck, in all its dented, faded glory, looked even worse for wear. Ajani announced that a volunteer doctor would come from Johannesburg with medical supplies. Nick rested easier that night, knowing that the dire needs would be met, the children wouldn't be hungry for long, and Lidiya would have a doctor here when she delivered her baby.

***

Nick stood by a fire and looked around at the reestablished camp. The weeks had gone quickly as they had rebuilt the refugee camp. Every donation and supply they could get their hands on were received gratefully, usually with tears. Ajani and Kofi were experts in making sure every resource was used wisely.

Nick had appreciated his time among these people, but it was time for him to return for council, and he wanted to meet with Allie beforehand. When it came time for Ajani to return the doctor to Johannesburg, Nick decided he would accompany them. He shook hands with and then embraced Ajani before joining the doctor on the bus. He knew his thoughts and concerns for the Ethiopian refugees would continue. He thought of Lidiya's baby born just a few weeks earlier. Lidiya named her Taraji, meaning hope. Such a miracle to witness the joy that her new baby brought in such dire circumstances. Nick watched as the bus doors closed, feeling the finality of his assignment.

CHAPTER 20

The serenity in the Time Room was a welcome reprieve but still felt odd coming from the rough conditions of the refugee camp. He walked to the entrance of the Rome library, checked the clock above the door, and entered.

This library had two large open rooms. The bookshelves were built into the walls, much like they were in the Time Room. On each of the four walls, there were rolling ladders that went along tracks about halfway up the shelves. There was a walkway at the top of the ladder that went the entire way around the room, with enough space for a person to grab a book and then head back down the ladder. In the center of each room were long tables, end to end, where library patrons could plug in a laptop or other device. There were a few people scattered throughout the library. The sounds of typing and book pages turning were the only interruptions to the silence. Nick headed straight for an office toward the back of the first open room.

Allie worked as a library curator. She had been there since the opening of this library. She'd taken a hiatus for a few decades so that no one would recognize that she wasn't aging and returned under a different name. Nick knocked on the mahogany door before pushing it open. The room was a chaotic mess of papers, maps, and books. Allie claimed it was perfectly organized, and that she knew exactly where everything was. Nick believed her. He closed the door quietly behind him.

"Allie?" Nick asked before approaching the desk and leaning around an enormous pile of books. It surprised him to see not one, but two people behind all the clutter.

"Jack!" Nick exclaimed. In a swift motion, Jack stood up from his crouched position next to Allie, who sat in her desk chair. Jack's head hit the corner of an open drawer in a file cabinet. A colorful word escaped Jack, and he quickly put one hand where he'd hit the cabinet and the other over his mouth. Allie and Nick exchanged an amused look.

"Are you okay, Jack?" Allie asked, her eyes scanning Jack's stance. She stood and closed the cabinet. Jack responded with a high-pitched mumble, his eyes squeezed shut. He took a breath before slowly opening his eyes again, blinking away tears. A sound in the corner drew Nick's attention away from his suffering friend. He looked down in time to see a silver cat leap from the ground to the top of the file cabinet that had been the source of Jack's language. It was a beautiful Persian cat, with long hair, perfectly groomed. The cat's squashed face gave it a very grumpy look.

"And who is this beauty?" Nick asked, reaching a hand out to stroke the cat's silky fur. He could feel the cat's purr as he ran his hand along its soft back.

"This is Cha-cha. I think you met her as a kitten."

"Of course," Nick said, trying to rack his brain. He'd met many of Allie's cats over the centuries. She'd always had one or more.

"Does the library allow cats?" Nick asked skeptically.

"Not technically, but as long as I keep her in the office, no one seems to mind, besides she helps keep away..." She clamped her mouth shut as if realizing she'd said too much. Nick assumed she was going to mention mice in the library and didn't want to press the issue. A slow exhale drew Nick's attention back to Jack.

"Sorry to surprise you. I thought you'd be in El Salvador."

"Mission accomplished. Now I'm back for the meeting tomorrow. How was Ethiopia?"

"The weather was the only good thing they had going for them, unfortunately. They were forced to move camp a few weeks into my stay there. The medical teams had to leave, and they lost a lot of what little they had. I stayed to help them get resettled and then came almost directly here."

"You have something in your teeth Nick – right there." She pointed at the spot on her own teeth. Nick picked at the spot with his fingernail but stopped when Allie let out a sharp gasp. "You brushed your teeth while you were in Ethiopia, right? I know it's harder when you're traveling, but you have to take care of your teeth. We may be eternal, but our bodies still need to be taken care of!" Her eyes were enormous behind her blue light glasses and the look of concern and accusation on her face made Nick wonder if this is what it would be like to have a mother, or perhaps an overprotective older sister. He threw his hands in front of him defensively.

"I brushed! I always do. Even before it became popular in the 1930s." He remembered the council meeting they had where Allie brought everyone toothbrushes and toothpaste for the first time.

"Right, well," Allie said, noticeably relaxing. "Sorry, I just volunteered over at the dentist's office here on Saturday. They clean teeth for those who can't afford insurance. Lots of homeless or jobless people came through and you wouldn't believe the things we saw," she said with a shudder. Allie had received many college degrees, including a dental degree. She enjoyed using it to help the less fortunate. She hadn't ever officially worked as a dentist aside from her time as an intern, but she was very passionate about dental hygiene as all the other protectors were well aware.

"I actually came for something specific," Nick said solemnly, changing the topic. Jack straightened his stance at the seriousness in Nick's voice.

"Have either of you been to the Time Room since our last council?" Nick asked. Allie shook her head.

"Only passing through to get here," Jack answered. Nick reached into his bag and pulled out the forbidden book. Allie gasped and put a hand over her mouth. Jack looked at her quizzically.

"That's... no, it can't be," she muttered. She looked between Nick and the book with wide eyes.

"You recognize it? You know where it's from?" Nick asked, surprised. She nodded.

"Does anyone want to clue me in? It looks like all the other old books in the Time Room to me." Allie hit his arm with the back of her hand.

"It isn't any other book. This one came from the sealed shelf."

Jack's gaze flew to Nick, who nodded once.

"What are you doing with that, Nick? Have you lost your mind? And how do you know that?" Jack rounded on Allie.

"Whoa, there Jack. I have studied all the books in the Time Room. It's kind of my job. I remember them all, including the covers of the ones on the sealed shelf. How did you get that, Nick?" Allie asked, brows furrowed.

"After the last council, I stayed in the council room to clean and meditate. As I was leaving, I heard a scuffle and a door slam. I didn't see who it was or what door they went through, but I noticed that someone had broken the bar across the sealed shelf. Someone shoved this book hastily back on the shelf.

"You took it?" Allie sounded horrified.

"Yes, I carried it with me to Ethiopia. I didn't open it without significant consideration and meditation," he said, hoping to settle their minds, though a part of his mind still pricked with guilt. "It didn't matter, anyway. I cannot read it." He reached the book toward Allie. She didn't take it, just looked.

"The Creator forbade this book, and its knowledge," she said firmly.

"Yes, but I can't believe it was a coincidence. The Shadow's voice in council, someone breaking the seal. It's all connected; I can feel it. We need to be prepared, and I feel the Creator brought about a means to prepare us by leading me to this book." Allie stood and closed her laptop and shuffled things around so she had an empty space in front of her. She sat down, reached out her hand and took the book from Nick, setting it on the desk in front of her. Jack leaned over to get a look at the cover.

"I don't recognize the language," Jack said, glancing up at Nick, who shrugged and looked back at Allie, who slowly opened the cover to the title page.

"It looks like languages I've seen before, maybe Aztec? Kaida would be the one to ask."

"I'll try to catch her after council tomorrow." Nick reached out for the book, but Allie didn't notice. She was flipping through the pages and running her hand along the words. She stopped when she came to the torn page.

"I guess we know what whoever did this was after. It looks like a map."

"What makes you say that?" Jack asked, coming around to her other side to get a better look. The area behind the desk felt crowded.

"This, up here in the corner." Allie pointed to the top right corner. "It looks like a legend, almost like they'd have on a map from the 15th century, and here." She pointed along the edge of the torn page. "This line looks like the edge of a land mass. It's just my best guess. Without knowing what the words say, it would be impossible to know." She closed the book and handed it back to Nick. She folded her arms underneath her cloak and rubbed her arms. "See what Kaida says," she said. The book felt somehow heavier as he placed it back in his bag, as if sharing the knowledge about the book made it more real, more daunting.

"Where are you staying tonight, Jack?" Nick asked, reaching to pet Cha-Cha again. She'd remained on top of the file cabinet, observing, her only movement the occasional flick of her tail.

"I hadn't thought that far ahead. What about you?" Jack said. This was the response Nick had expected from his spontaneous friend.

"I have a hotel room close to the New York library. You're welcome to stay with me. I'm going to rest. The time change is taking its toll," Nick said, changing his watch to match New York time again, even though he was in Rome. Maybe it was time to upgrade to an electric watch that automatically adjusted to the different time zones. Or not. This watch had served him well and kept him connected to the watch shop he liked so much in Germany.

"That sounds great. Leave the address and I'll catch up with you later." Nick wrote it down and said his goodbyes. He looked over his shoulder as he left the office and saw Jack leaning over Allie to point to something on her desk. Her blush was obvious. Nick smiled to himself. He was happy to leave the two of them to each other until tomorrow.

CHAPTER 21

Nick awoke to sunlight streaming through the gaps of the curtains of his hotel room. The soft snoring from the bed next to his reminded him he had a roommate. Jack had come to the hotel late the night before. He had entered with his normal exuberance and began talking a million miles a minute. He told Nick about going to dinner with Allie and walking around the Botanical Garden of Rome. When Nick said it sounded like a significant date, Jack was quick to shut him down, insisting they were just friends. Nick saw through his feeble attempt at denial, but let it slide. He'd enjoy watching this all play out.

Nick stood, stretched his arms above his head, and looked out the window down at the street below. Last night, the sidewalks buzzed with people heading out for the night. This morning, being Saturday, there was hardly anyone. He headed to the bathroom to shower and change. Jack didn't stir as Nick moved about the room. Nick would see if he wanted to grab some of the hotel's complimentary breakfast when he finished. After his short, lukewarm shower, he came out to find Jack sitting on the edge of his bed, flipping through the ancient book.

"Hey, I hope you don't mind. I grabbed this from your bag." Jack looked up guiltily. "Well, the wind grabbed it for me. I wasn't snooping, I promise." He grimaced as Nick rolled his eyes. "I am just curious... Why this book? What was worth breaking the seal for? Who do you think did this?"

"I have my suspicions, but I'd like to gather more facts first," Nick answered.

"Hmmm," Jack hummed absentmindedly, shutting the book and setting it on the bed. He stood, stretching just as Nick had. These beds couldn't claim comfort, but it was better than the ground, or trying to sleep on a chair in the council room. He'd done both many times. "Let me get cleaned up and we can head down to breakfast. I hope this place has crepes."

"Not the last time I stayed, but they have those waffle things where you cook it yourself and flip it over halfway," Nick said.

"Nice," Jack said, disappearing into the bathroom. Nick picked up the book from the bed and returned it to his bag. Jack's voice echoed in his mind. *Who do you think did this?*

***

Full of waffles, Jack and Nick headed through the New York library and into the Time Room. Allie was setting out bottles of water at each desk when they walked in.

"Hey guys," she said shyly, looking at Jack. Nick glanced at his watch. There were still a few hours left before council was scheduled to start. He grabbed a handful of American money out of an envelope on Allie's board and tucked it into his bag. He looked at the board to see if there were any other notes or notices applicable to him. Not seeing anything new, he reread an older announcement. It was about a new policy abroad that would affect some international travel. He took the pin out of the note, confident everyone had received the message. It was most likely posted by Allie right around the time of the change. As he crumpled up the note and looked around for a trash can, he had an idea.

"I'm going to go check on someone. I'll be back for council." Jack and Allie were deep in conversation and barely acknowledged his comment. Jack opened the door to the New York library and traced his steps from a few months back. A half hour later, he stood in front of the homeless shelter where Nick and Jack had dropped off Calvin. He pushed the door open and heard an electric beep announcing his presence. A woman at the front desk stood in greeting. A security guard tensed by the door.

"Hello, may I help you?" the woman asked politely.

"My friend and I brought a man here a few months ago. I'm wondering if you have any information on him?"

"What kind of information?" she asked suspiciously. "Do you have a warrant?" Nick raised his eyebrows in confusion. Was his cloak portraying him as a police officer? Unfortunately, there were no reflective surfaces for him to casually check.

"No, no, nothing like that!" Nick said with a laugh, and the woman seemed to visibly relax. "His name is Calvin, and I was just wondering - did he stay more than one night? Did he get the help he needed?"

"You must mean Cal!" the receptionist said brightly. "That sweetheart!" She sat back down and beckoned Nick to approach the desk. "I can't share any confidential information, of course, unless you have a warrant or social security documentation?" Nick shook his head.

"I can tell you he stayed with us for a few nights and then was taken to a rehab center by his daughter," she said in a low voice, like she didn't want to be overheard.

"His daughter?" Nick said, surprised, unable to keep the corners of his lips from turning up.

"Yes, it was quite the emotional reunion. I have heard nothing since. Is there anything else I can help you with?" she asked. Nick paused before answering.

"No, thank you. It sounds like he is in excellent hands."

"I see many people in and out of these shelter doors, and I agree. He seemed genuinely interested in change and in being a good father and grandfather again." The door opened behind him and a man and woman dressed in rags stumbled through the door with a small dog on a leash. The woman behind the desk rose to her feet again.

"Thank you for speaking with me." He glanced at the couple that had just entered. They were having a lively discussion with the security guard about the dog. The woman was determined that the dog should be allowed to stay with them. Her conviction would be admirable if not for her own obviously dire situation. He cleared his throat and turned his attention back to the receptionist. "I have a cash donation for the shelter. Can I give that to you?"

"Yes, thank you sir, um, let me see if this couple is staying and then I'll get a form and envelope for you." She made her way around the desk but stopped as the homeless woman began shouting.

"If she can't stay, then neither will we!" The homeless woman stormed out, the man close on her heels. The door slammed closed behind them and the electronic beep of the door sounded weak in the awkward silence that filled the room.

"Okay then, never mind," the receptionist said. "You'd be surprised at how often that happens." She fished an envelope and form out from a drawer in her desk and Nick filled it out. Nick took a hundred-dollar bill out of the pile he'd brought and put the rest into the envelope for the shelter. After thanking her, he hurriedly went outside. He reached out with his power to find the turbulent conviction and determination of the woman and followed. He walked down the road and into an alley near where he and Jack had found Calvin. The homeless couple were settling down for the night in a shabby makeshift tent. Other tents were set up in the alleyway, but all the tenants kept to themselves.

The man and woman didn't see or hear him approach. They were arranging blankets and straightening their tent. The small terrier sniffed around the outside of a nearby dumpster. Nick leaned down and tucked the hundred-dollar bill into its threadbare collar. The dog was clearly too tired and too downtrodden to bark. Nick rubbed the dog behind the ear, then left as swiftly as he'd come, not wanting to cause a scene. He knew full well that they might not use the money for food or clothing, but at least they had the option. He stopped frequently on his way back to the Library. There was still plenty of time before council. Each time he passed a homeless soul along his path, he stopped to talk. Well, more like he stopped to listen. It was amazing how much these people, sitting in such desperation, were keen to open up when they had a willing listener. One man ended their visit with a prayer. His sweet words to the Creator filled his soul with faith and hope in humanity. He wished he could walk each person he sat with to the shelter and get them the help they needed, but he followed the lead of the Creator. He knew these people better than anyone. The Creator knew what they needed, when they needed it, and what it would take for them to find that help. No two journeys are the same.

CHAPTER 22

Allie and Jack were still the only ones in the Time Room when Nick returned just in time for council. As Nick entered, Jack took a small step away from Allie and looked around the room self-consciously.

"Did everything go well?" Allie asked kindly. Before Nick could answer her, their attention was drawn to the council room door. They had heard a door slam and heels clicking across the Time Room floor. Kaida rushed into the room.

"I only have forty minutes before my next meeting. It's in Arlington." She glanced at her watch, mumbling as she did the math backwards of when she'd need to leave and still be close to on time.

"We're just waiting for Ben," Allie said as Kaida sat at her desk, perched on the edge of her office chair, as if sitting comfortably would make the meeting last longer. They waited another five minutes, but Kaida's impatience was contagious.

"Let's get started and Ben can join us. I just want to know if any of you have seen any repercussions of the Shadow's message to us? Have you noticed any shifts in human behaviors? Any disrupts in weather patterns or natural disasters?" Nick asked. "Kaida, any thoughts?" Kaida stood at her desk, her golden cloak glimmering in the room's lighting. She glanced at her watch before answering.

"It's hard to say. I've been trying to keep my eyes and ears open, as always, but I can't say I've noticed a specific shift. Corruption still runs rampant in global, national, and local politics, of course, but that's nothing new. All I can do is try to encourage the right people into the right places. So, I guess my answer is no. What about you, Allie?" Allie blinked rapidly as the attention suddenly shifted to her.

"I guess I would say the same. I've kept to my little corner of the world and haven't noticed a difference." She shrugs and then adds, "Oh wait, there was a surge in family history names being researched and documented. There was a new software developed that makes uploading the documents easier and a historian organization just found some war records from the late 1800s. History nerds like me have been devouring the records, making them accessible to all countries so people can find the names of their ancestors. If they can find where they served and when, they can connect them to other people they served with. Really, it's not such a large world. Especially once you go back a few generations. You can have neighbors living right next to each other that share similar ancestors without even knowing it. The other day in the library I saw an elderly woman trying to look up her grandfather's military records and guess who was helping her learn the computer program? Her granddaughter. My eyes started to tear up. It was the most beautiful..." She trailed off when she saw Kaida again looking at her watch. "Oh, sorry." She sat down, looking surprised at her own torrent of words. It wasn't often she became so passionate.

"Jack?" Nick asked. Jack had been staring open-mouthed at Allie's flood of information. No doubt surprised by her excitement. She was always so timid and shy.

"Just the hurricane in the Midwest United States and flooding in Vietnam. Those aren't unusual. I'm actually headed to Australia after this. They have another wildfire that is raging. I was going to go help get that under control. Directing the wind can make a huge difference in containment. I'll get to wear their amazing fire and rescue uniform again. Neon looks good on me." He smirked, then looked to the door of the council room. "Where is Benny?" Everyone ignored his use of the detested nickname.

"If he's not here by now, he probably isn't coming." Kaida said, "I'm sorry. I can't wait. Should we just plan on meeting again at the yearly council meeting? I really don't have time to squeeze in extra meetings." She stood and turned to the door. Her shoes clicked across the floor again as she dashed from the room, not waiting for an answer.

"People need to stop leaving this way," Nick muttered. He suddenly remembered the book from the shelf. Swiftly rising from his seat, he ran after Kaida. He caught her with her hand on the door to the Washington, D.C. library.

"Kaida, I had a question really quickly," Nick said. Kaida glanced at her watch and then back to Nick, eyebrows raised, impatience etched in her features. She didn't remove her hand from the door to the library. "It's..." Nick's words stopped in his throat. He felt as though a hand were pressing into his chest, lungs constricted. He couldn't breathe. A pounding pressure pulsed in his head, and the room spun. Then it was gone. Kaida looked at him curiously.

"Are you okay?" she asked sincerely, stepping away from the door and placing a hand on his arm, trying to look up into his eyes.

"Uh, yes," Nick said, breathing hard. He looked at Kaida cautiously, as his breathing returned to normal.

"What did you need to ask me? I have a cab waiting outside the library," Kaida said, taking a step back toward the door and placing her hand back on the doorknob.

"Nothing. It's not important. Sorry to delay you. Thank you for your insight today."

Kaida nodded. The corner of her cloak glinted as it disappeared just before the door slammed shut. Nick leaned against the wall next to the door. He placed a hand on his chest, rubbing away some of the muscle tension.

Allie and Jack exited the council room together, Allie laughing at something Jack had said. She stopped immediately when she saw

Nick leaning against the wall. Jack rushed forward. "Nick, are you alright?"

"Yes, just a strange experience is all." He turned to Allie. "I don't think Kaida can help me. Will you give me the contact information for the man you think can translate the book?"

"Of course, you're still rather pale. Do you need to rest?" Allie asked.

"I'll rest on my journey. This is too important."

"I'll need to go to my office at the library to find his contact information."

"Thank you. I'll find one of Ben's hawks and get a message to him. It's not like him to miss a council." Nick pushed off the wall and walked back into the council room. He pulled a paper and pen from his bag, scrawled a quick note to Ben and placed it in a thick envelope from his desk drawer. He walked around the circular room to the New Zealand library entrance. The clock above the door showed it was ten in the morning there. He walked through and heard a boisterous reader and the voices of many small children. He looked around a bookshelf and saw parents lined up along the side wall, whispering to each other or watching the librarian read. A dozen children sat on the floor, the older ones listening to the story, the smaller ones rolling around, wiggling, or in their mother's arms. He moved inconspicuously and exited the side door. He walked around and entered the forested area behind the library. His eyes scanned the skies as he walked. He heard an owl's distinct hoot and saw a few rainbirds pass overhead, but no hawks. He stood still, watching and waiting, then continued further into the forest. Finally, he heard the distinct call of a hawk. He followed the sound and watched as a hawk lighted from the branch of a miro tree, circled over his head a few times and then swooped down to land on his shoulder.

"Hello there. You seem familiar," Nick said, looking at the large bird from the corner of his eye. He reached a hand out and handed the hawk his message. "This is for Ben. We're concerned. Leave your response near the library and Allie will collect it." Nick wasn't sure if the bird understood all of his words, but Ben would get the message. With a squeeze to his shoulder and a shift of its weight, the hawk took off toward Ben's cabin. Nick watched for as long as he could and then found his way back through the forest to the library and back to the Time Room. Allie and Jack stood waiting. Allie handed Nick a sticky note with a name and address scribbled across it.

"Daniel Wilhelmus Via A. Fortini 26, Assisi"

"I met him," Allie explained, "when we were both working on a project at Sapienza University. He's since retired and lives in Assisi. It's just under two hours, if you travel by train. I looked up train times and wrote those on the note as well." Nick looked down at the note, then looked at the clock above the door to the Rome library. He'd have to hurry to catch the first train.

"Thank you," Nick said, looking once more at his friends. He rushed through the door to the Rome library.

CHAPTER 23

He missed the first train. Nick found a bench at the station and looked at his ticket. He'd have to wait an hour and twenty minutes before the next train to Assisi. He worked to tame his irritation and instead took to people watching. Most of the people at this time of day were either weekend workers or people heading out for the night. He could detect a handful of students from the local university as well; the backpacks were usually a good indicator. Both the students and workers carried an aura of weariness. Nick noticed two students engaged in a deep discussion about an art project they had been assigned. He enjoyed the fervor and passion in their conversation. Suddenly, his attention shifted to an elderly woman sitting on a bench across the station from him. A man in a fine suit sat next to her, looking at his phone. He narrowed in on the emotions of the older woman – content with a hint of loneliness. Nick wondered where she was traveling to and why she was alone. Thanks to his missed train, he had time. He crossed the station, being careful not to walk too quickly. He didn't wish to alarm anyone. As he approached the older woman, she looked up at him with hopeful eyes. The man on his phone didn't react at all.

"Sir, do you mind if I take this seat here?" Nick pointed to the small space between him and the older woman. The man looked at Nick, confused. Nick just waited for it to click. Clearly, Nick wouldn't fit into that space and was asking the man to move.

"Oh, right, of course," the man said, finally catching on. He moved to sit on a different bench before continuing to scroll on his phone. Nick took the man's seat, his knees turned toward the older woman. He could feel her amusement at the exchange and her face held a warm smile.

"And how are you today, young man?" the woman asked. Nick smiled to himself. If only she knew he'd lived over a dozen of her lifetimes.

"I am well, just waiting for a train as the rest of us are. How are you?"

"Just dandy. It's such a lovely winter day." The woman adjusted the knitted wool scarf around her neck.

"Did you make that scarf?" Nick asked, small talk seeming the way to go.

"Oh yes, one of my many old woman hobbies. When you get to be my age, you find ways to keep your mind sharp and your hands busy."

"An admirable pastime. I like to work with wood occasionally. Like you said, keeping my hands busy," Nick shared.

"How wonderful. My husband liked to carve as well, always as a hobby, of course. I would say, 'Open a shop! Do what you love!' but he would just laugh it off and insist he had to stay in his day job to pay the bills. At his funeral four years ago, I had two entire tables displaying his small carvings, bowls and little figures, even a few toys he'd made for our grandchildren. That's who I'm going to see today. It's so much easier for me to get on a train to visit them than it is for my son and his wife to bring their four children here. I've got to take advantage of my mobility while I have it. Those grandkids do wonders for keeping me young." The woman's eyes were bright as she spoke of her family.

"Tell me more about your grandkids," Nick prompted. She looked surprised, but pleased.

"The boys are teenagers now and are very into sports and video games. They do well in school and I'm so proud of them. Then the family was surprised with twin girls. They'll be four this year and are so active! All of them are such a joy to be around."

"Have you considered moving closer to them?" Nick asked. She looked at him sharply, a hint of suspicion in her eyes.

"We discussed the possibility of moving in with them just last week," she paused. Nick said nothing, waiting for her to continue. "I just don't know. I've lived here in Rome my entire married life. What would I do in Florence? I don't know anyone there and the last thing I'd want to do is to be a burden to anyone." Nick heard and felt the sincerity of her words.

"Change is hard, but something tells me you would be much more help than a burden."

"You think so?" she asked, turning her body more toward Nick, leaning forward slightly.

"Absolutely. Grandmothers are one of the most treasured loves a child can have. You should be by those rapscallions." He smiled mischievously, and the woman giggled. "Of course, these are all the opinions of a stranger," Nick said.

"A kind stranger that could just be the angel I needed, in the right place at the right time," she said with a smile. Nick shrugged, then listened to the announcement of a train. "That's my train," the woman said, using a cane to help her stand. Nick stood up too, offering his hand in case she required assistance. "Thank you for joining me and for the lovely chat. I was feeling lonely. I'm Lucia, by the way," she said, shifting her cane to her left hand and reaching out with her right.

"Nick," he said, taking her hand. "Have a safe journey and enjoy your time with family."

"Thank you." Nick watched as she headed to her train. Wondering if he should've offered to walk with her, but thinking better of it. Her independence was important to her. He hoped she found a way to maintain that and be close to her family. He looked at the large clock on the wall and headed back toward where his train would arrive soon.

***

Nick checked the address on the sticky note from Allie before raising his hand to knock on the door of the small two-story townhome. The welcome mat crunched lightly under his feet as he turned around and admired the view from the front steps. Stone buildings lined the streets; cold, shriveled vines climbed most of the buildings, making Nick think this street would be most beautiful in the spring. The clear blue sky and the crisp air helped him feel lighter despite the heaviness of his task.

"Can I help you?" Nick heard a woman ask behind him. He turned around and met the eyes of a full-bodied older woman. Her white hair was perfectly coiffed, her green dress was wrinkle free, and she had a simple strand of pearls around her neck. She studied him expectantly and he offered a reassuring smile. Nick could feel her curiosity and nervousness.

"Hello, are you Mrs. Wilhelmus?"

"I am," she said, still guarded.

"My name is Nick. I'm wondering if I could speak with your husband. Is he home?" He was proud of himself for remembering to add the question. He could sense another person in the house, but she didn't know that.

Mrs. Wilhelmus stepped out onto the covered porch and closed the door behind her. She wrapped her arms around herself defensively, against Nick or the cold. He wasn't sure. Perhaps both. "Is this about an artifact? A translation? Some kind of archeology project or a discovered ancient rune?" She asked each question harshly, becoming quieter with each question. Nick felt the building turmoil within the woman and decided a direct approach would be best.

"Yes. It's a translation. An important one that I hear your husband may be able to help me with."

"I worried it would be something like that. I must ask you to leave." She gripped her arms even tighter around her middle. Nick took a half step back. He could feel the woman's resolve mixed in with a hint of fear and exasperation.

"Please, it's very important," Nick said sincerely.

"That's what they all say," she snapped. "My husband sits and stews all day long. Thinking and rethinking every project he's ever worked on. He's a shell of a person, haunted by unfinished works and unanswered questions. I can't put him through any more. He's old. We're *retired,* for heaven's sake. Please, let us enjoy what small portion of this life we have left to live in peace." She opened her door and turned around to close it with Nick still outside. He thought quickly and reached out his hand to stop the door.

"I may be able to help," he said.

"I seriously doubt that. The best thing you can do for him is leave and don't come back. Please don't make me call the Polizia."

"Hear me out. I believe this project could give him the peace of mind you are hoping for." It was more likely Nick could provide him with the peace he needed. "I've seen it work before. I sense you are good people and I'd like to help." The woman stared at him a moment longer. She sighed and opened the door.

"Very well, but we have a lunch appointment in an hour, so keep it brief. He's in his office, as usual." She led him past a narrow staircase and around a corner to a small office. She lifted her hand and knocked quickly as she turned the handle and entered. Nick's eyes met an older man, stooped with age, his white hair thinning on top. Glasses sat on the end of his nose and he shuffled papers back and forth across the desk, muttering to himself. Nick could feel just as strongly as he could see the man's discontent. The woman cleared her throat.

"Not now, Beatrice. I'm busy," he said with a wave of his hand, not looking up. Mrs. Wilhelmus didn't seem taken aback by his rudeness. She must have become used to this side of him in their many years of marriage.

"You have a visitor," she huffed. The man behind the desk finally looked up, papers still clutched in each hand. His glasses nearly slipped off his nose at the sudden movement. His bushy eyebrows furled, meeting in the middle.

"I'll leave you to it. Don't forget Daniel, lunch with Ricci at noon." Daniel stared at Nick, then gestured for him to sit in the chair across from his desk. He watched Nick sit and then carefully set aside the papers he'd been shuffling through. He leaned back in his chair, adjusted his sweater and looked over the top of his glasses at Nick.

"You don't look like a scholar or a historian. Why are you here?" he asked. Nick wondered how he appeared to this man and what a historian would look like. The only historian he knew was Allie, and he just knew her in her ivory cloak.

"My name is Nick. My friend Allie has sent me from Rome. You worked with her at the university."

"Allie?" He paused, thinking. Then his eyes lit up. "Allie, of course! How wonderful! How is she? It's been years! Such a joy to work with, so insightful. I swear that woman could remember everything from the beginning of time." Nick smiled at how true the statement was.

"She is well and sends her warmest regards. She sent me to you because I've come across a book. It's in a language that I can't translate. Allie wasn't confident in her ability to translate it. I was wondering if you'd look at it with me." Nick pulled the book from his bag. He could feel the man's excitement building. He hesitated before handing the book to Daniel. "I can provide you with very little information about the book's past, and I must insist that you discuss it with no one else. Do I have your word?"

"Yes, yes, of course," Daniel said, reaching his hand forward. His words may have sounded flippant, but Nick felt the sincerity. He handed the book to Daniel and watched as he pushed the glasses up his nose and ran a hand softly over the ancient cover. He flipped through silently and carefully, page after page. Nick waited patiently, recognizing this to be a part of Daniel's process and not wanting to interrupt. When he got to the torn page, he huffed.

"Such damage to such an old book. Shameful." Nick nodded his agreement and Daniel continued, "Translating this book correctly could take years."

"What about the torn page? Could you translate just those words at the top?"

The room again fell silent as Daniel turned back to the torn page. His eyes scanned the words, he leaned closer to the book and then further, as if trying to get it to come into focus.

"It seems to be a cross between Egyptian and Hebrew. Like this hieroglyph here in the corner. It appears to be the symbol for hope, but it has an extra little swoop here. That resembles the hieroglyphic for truth. It could be both, and once I dive deeper into the written language here, it will give me a better understanding of the words." Nick felt his own excitement building alongside Daniel's.

"So, you can translate it?" Nick asked eagerly. Daniel took his glasses off and rubbed his eyes with the heels of his hands.

"Yes," he said slowly, and Nick's heart quickened.

"I can pay you," Nick offered quickly.

"We can discuss that later. Will you be staying in Assisi this week? I don't have time to work this out today and really, it could take a few days."

"I will stay in town. There's a hotel just around the corner. I'd like to keep the book with me. Can we copy the page for translating?"

"Of course," Daniel replied. Nick opened the torn page and Daniel took it to the printer in the office's corner. Daniel gently and expertly handled the book so as not to damage the spine or any pages as it scanned. The sound of the printer filled the office. The door opened and Beatrice poked her head in.

"Danny, we need to get ready to go," she insisted.

"No problem. I was just leaving. When can I check back in with you?" Nick asked. Daniel handed the book back to Nick.

"I can call you when I'm done or if I need to see more of the book for reference."

"No need, I'll drop by," Nick said, knowing that not having a cell phone would make it difficult for Daniel to get hold of him. He had no intention of sitting around next to his hotel room phone for a call. Daniel paused and looked at Nick strangely. Nick kept his face neutral.

"Okay then. I'll see you later... at some unknown time... when you'll just drop by," Daniel said slowly, looking at Nick over the top of his glasses. Nick nodded and showed himself to the door.

He could feel Beatrice and Daniel's confusion. The completion of the translation was the only thing that mattered.

CHAPTER 24

The closest hotel was very old but decently maintained and most importantly - clean. He opted to take the stairs instead of the rickety elevator up to his assigned room. Instead of laying down on the bed as he had planned, Nick picked up his staff and headed outside. Indoors still felt strange after spending the past few months outdoors or in a tent. He walked along the streets toward the center of town. His staff made a satisfying click against the stone pathways. Stone buildings towered all around him and he noticed empty flower pots on almost every set of stairs he passed, whether a home or a shop. Once again, he thought how beautiful it must be in Assisi in the spring. As it was, he was grateful for the warmth of his cloak in the January cold. He passed a small shop with a man on a ladder, removing Christmas lights from the awning over the store window.

"Hello, sir!" the man called down from the ladder. "Would you mind handing me that hammer? I've got a nail that won't come loose up here." Nick picked up the hammer and handed it to the man on the ladder, wishing him a good day, before continuing on his way.

Nick came to what he thought must be a town square park: a square of grass with a few scattered benches. A memorial stone in one corner of the square honored the town's founders. In the very center of the grass, lit up with a solar powered spotlight, were carved wooden statues of three men. Nick walked closer to admire the workmanship. The statues were roughly six feet tall, carved from cedar wood, each holding a gift. Nick remembered these men, their studying, searching, and eventual finding. He admired their dedication and understanding of the importance of their role in this earth's story. A sign carved out of the same wood as the three statues read, "Wise Men Still Seek Him" with some Bible verses underneath. He contemplated the wisdom of these words until a car pulled up to the small square. A man turned off the car, and a woman began unloading kids from the back of the vehicle. Time for Nick to go. He walked back to the hotel, noticing the lights successfully removed from the store he'd passed earlier, no ladder in sight.

Politely nodding to the woman behind the service desk, he entered the hotel and made his way to his room. He looked at the phone on the bedside table, then shook his head. He'd call Allie in the morning.

***

Nick woke late the next morning, not feeling a need to set an alarm. He rolled into a sitting position and rubbed the sleep from his eyes. Picking up the phone, he dialed the memorized number to Allie's office at the Rome Library. It rang three times and just as Nick was thinking how she probably wasn't in the office because it was Sunday, the fifth ring was interrupted.

"Hello?" Allie's familiar voice asked over the phone, sounding slightly breathless.

"Allie, it's Nick. Are you okay?"

"Yes, I just heard the phone ringing as I came in to grab something and rushed before I missed it. I, uh, tripped over a pile of books, which didn't help the rushing situation," she finished, and Nick was sure if he could see Allie, he'd see color in her cheeks.

"I was just checking in to see if you had heard from Ben?" Nick asked.

"No, I checked where the hawks usually leave notes in New Zealand this morning and there was nothing. I think it might be too soon though. He could've been away from his house when his hawk arrived, or a million other things."

"True. Thank you for checking. Can you call this number back if you hear anything? If I'm not around, you can leave a discreet message with the front desk."

"How is Daniel?"

"He said 'hello' and spoke fondly of working with you. He seems…" Nick searched for the right word, "distracted. Discontent, maybe. There are a lot of warring emotions in him, and he seems unable to settle any of them. But he's confident he'll be able to translate at least one page of the book for me in the next few days."

"I'm glad he can help. Do you think you can help him in return? He was always so kind to me," Allie reflected.

"I'll do what I can," Nick assured her before hanging up.

***

Nick turned the corner toward the Wilhelmus's door. Beatrice was out front pulling dead plants from flower pots and heard him approach. She wore a thick coat, winter hat, and garden gloves.

"Hello, Mrs. Wilhelmus. I've come to see if Daniel needs any help. May I go in?"

"You certainly may not." The irritation in her voice surprised Nick. "He has been awake all night with his nose in that page you gave him, muttering to himself and making notes. He never came to bed last night and this morning I found him asleep at his desk. I woke him just a few minutes ago and sent him to get some rest. He'll be out for another few hours, we'll miss church, I'd imagine." Nick was happy to know he'd worked on translating, but felt guilty at the pointed look Beatrice gave him. She had said this might happen, and it was the reason she had almost sent him away yesterday.

"I'm sorry, Mrs. Wilhelmus. I know this isn't what you wanted. What he's working on is very important, I promise." Nick felt a wave of sadness from Beatrice.

"Important. Of course. Come back in a few hours," she said, turning back to her flower pots.

"I will, thank you." Nick took a few steps down the road and then turned. Mrs. Wilhelmus was sitting back on her heels, her hands in her lap, staring into the flowerpot in front of her. Nick knew he could help them. The overwhelming sadness and loneliness he sensed from Beatrice was interwoven with the disappointment she felt. Nick was sure she had imagined a stress-free retirement, finally spending time with her husband without the pressures of work. Instead, he'd held onto that work, obsessing over unsolved projects.

He entered the hotel and was stopped just as he approached the doors of the elevator.

"Mr. Smith." He turned to see the woman behind the desk standing and waving him over. She looked as old as Nick often felt. She had pulled back her gray hair into a tight bun, which suited her no-nonsense persona. The wrinkles around her eyes and mouth were as deep as some of the grooves in the weathered desk she stood behind.

"Yes?" Nick asked, approaching the desk.

"A call came for you while you were out. I have a message for you. Though it might be nonsense." She pushed a notecard across the counter to Nick. The hotel's logo was embossed on the top.

"Nick, no hawk has landed. The weather remains cold. Frosty agrees that a visit may be required. He is heading to Australia and will remain until he hears otherwise. Cheers, Allie."

Nick scowled at the note. When he looked up, the concierge hastily looked down. He sensed her slight embarrassment and curiosity. He'd have to leave her curious.

"Thank you for passing this along," he acknowledged. She nodded stiffly, and Nick continued to his room. He set his bag down on the bed and walked from one side of the small room to the other. His hands clasped behind his back as he paced. Why hadn't Ben responded? Did he need help? Had he received their message? Something about this wasn't sitting right. Ben had never enjoyed council, but he'd never completely skipped it. He'd never exploded on any of the other protectors before. They always valued his wisdom, and he did so much for this world and the earth itself. Was the increasing evil adding to his own physical stress? They were all feeling the strain, but was it something more? Was his connection with the earth being compromised? No, that wasn't possible. Was it? Was Ben pulling back from the others a sign of something deeper? Darker? He didn't mention going on a mission anywhere and if he was home, why wouldn't he respond? Had he gone off the grid somewhere more remote than his cottage? He would surely leave a note on Allie's board or send a hawk.

Nick's thoughts continued to roil. As he turned from his pacing, he glanced at the bed and saw the ancient book. He stopped short, his heart rate increasing. What if Ben's flighty exit had been a ruse? He could easily have left and returned after everyone else, not knowing Nick had stayed behind. Nick's concern deepened as he resumed pacing, considering Ben's behavior. He had to speak with Ben. His stomach grumbled and Nick remembered a cafe he'd passed while wandering the streets the night before.

The same stern woman behind the desk bid him a good day as he exited through the lobby. He turned left toward the busier part of town and began his search. As he approached a corner of two busy streets, he looked across and saw the charming little building. Its red and white striped awnings and the word 'café' elegantly swirled across the front window called to his empty stomach.

He opened the front door to the chime of a bell, not a mechanical beep as was so common in most parts of the world these days, but actual jingle bells that hung from the inside handle of the door. Glancing around the café, there were a few people scattered throughout the room enjoying cups of coffee and light conversation. His eyes connected with a curly haired woman at the corner booth and he nodded politely before turning to look at the menu. Hoping to enjoy a peaceful lunch, he intentionally pushed away the emotions of those in the cafe. He stepped closer to look at the display of confectionaries in the glass case. An éclair with raspberries across the top caught his eye. Not for himself, but perhaps as a peace offering for Mrs. Wilhelm. He ordered the éclair from a young woman with short blonde hair and a nose ring. Then he ordered an egg and tomato tramezzino for himself.

As he waited for his order, the energy of the room shifted. His shield against the emotions in the room fell, and he became hyper aware of each person in the cafe. One person stood out. He remained facing the counter as he felt a rage building within a woman behind him. It started as surprise, then moved to irritation, but the emotion grew harder and harsher as he stood waiting. This rage was dangerous. His hand tightened on his staff, his knuckles turning white. He looked out of the corner of his eye to the source of this raw emotion and froze when he saw the woman with the curly hair in the corner booth staring daggers at him. He barely had time to register her laptop and coffee before turning back toward the barista.

"Your order," she said, pushing a red tray with the éclair and sandwich on it across the counter to him.

"Thank you," he managed as he took the tray. The emotion grew stronger, and he heard footsteps approach behind him. Nick braced himself for the boiling rage to be released.

"Mi ignorerai e basta? Come osi?! E proprio oggi!" the woman shouted. Nick turned around and slowly raised his head to meet her angry gaze. He could feel the eyes of everyone in the cafe.

"I'm sorry, I don't speak Italian," he said softly, his words laced with regret.

"Oh!" the woman said with a deep blush. Nick felt her rage fade almost as quickly as it had built. "I thought you were... Oh, never mind. Please forgive me." She stuttered, turning back to her table, clearly mortified. She slammed her laptop shut and shoved it into her bag. In her rush to escape, her hands shook. She hit her coffee cup harder than intended, tipping it over and sending coffee rushing over the edge of the table, dripping to the floor. The blonde woman behind the counter grabbed a rag and hurried over, but Nick got there first. He used the pile of napkins on his tray to stop the brown liquid from streaming to the floor, then stepped aside and let the barista take over.

"I'm so sorry," the woman repeated, doing her best to move things out of the way as the barista cleaned up the spill.

"It happens," was the barista's only response. The woman gathered her bag and sent an apologetic look at Nick before turning toward the door.

"Ma'am, stop." She paused, looking ready to run. "Would you care to join me?"

"I..." Whatever excuse she was cooking died on her lips when Nick turned and ordered her another coffee. Almost as if in a trance, she followed Nick to another table and sat across from him, setting her bag down on the bench next to her. She placed her elbows on the table and placed her forehead on her hands, her brown curls falling in front of her face. Everyone in the café returned their attention to wherever it was before this woman's explosion and the soft din of conversation continued.

"Sir, I am so sorry. I've never lost it on anyone like that before. I don't know what came over me."

"May I know your name?" he asked gently. She didn't look up from the table.

"Aurora," she mumbled.

"I'm Nick."

Aurora laughed to herself. "I'm so embarrassed. Yelling at you like that. I just thought…" Nick held up his hand to stop her.

"Let's start with, I forgive you. Now, who did you think I was?" Nick asked, taking a bite of his sandwich.

"I thought you were Antonio's… dad," she said, looking up guiltily at Nick through her fingers. "Which is ridiculous. You are not nearly old enough. It must have been the lighting, and…"

"The white hair," Nick said, running a hand through his defining feature. "Don't worry. It happens all the time. Tell me more about Antonio," Nick said, taking another bite of his sandwich.

"You are American?" she asked.

"I am," Nick said. Though he'd lived in many countries throughout his life, it seemed like the simplest answer.

"You do not live here?"

"No. I am here only for a small project and then will return home." Aurora looked at him and then took a large breath, letting it out slowly. Nick felt her skepticism turn to calm before she began her story.

"Seven years ago, I dated a man, Antonio. We met in college. I instantly felt drawn to him. Love at first sight. He was the one. The man I was going to marry. Luckily, he agreed with me," she said with a small laugh. "We were engaged and very much in love. He worked in the next town over and I worked here as a tour guide for all the visitors we get. I still do. It is my second love." She paused. Her eyes glazed momentarily, lost in a memory. "One day on his drive home, there was a terrible storm. Snow isn't common here, so we have little practice driving in it. He was in a hurry to make it back in time to watch a soccer game with me. He hit a patch of ice and was in a head on crash. Antonio… died. I never saw him again." She paused, collecting herself. "I did not attend the funeral. I couldn't." Nick felt her remorse in full force. "Today would have been his thirty-fifth birthday. All day I have imagined what our lives would've been like. Maybe some kids, a nice little townhome with a view, and our own little family traditions. Oh, the possibilities! I will never know. When you walked into the cafe, I could have sworn you were his father. Despite being together so long, I only met him a handful of times and that was years ago. They never reached out after his death. I guess I never did either. I couldn't believe that he would walk into a café, look straight at me, and then pretend he didn't know who I was. It seemed too coincidental, today of all days."

"No need to apologize, and there are no coincidences."

"I believe you are right. I had no one to talk to about Antonio today, or no one I would talk about him with. Somehow everyone thinks I need to just move on and when I bring him up, they think I am living in the past. Perhaps I am. I am trying to move on. I've even dated a little, but it all seems so forced." She looked up, seeming surprised at her own words. "Anyway, thank you for listening, and being the one I could tell. Someone I could dump all this on and not worry about you judging me, because you don't know me or Antonio, someone so outside of the situation that it was easy to let it all out. Thank you."

"My pleasure. Aurora, your pain is your own, as is your grief. No one gets to take that away from you. There is no timeline. Occasionally, in the heavens, two masses collide, causing them to be temporarily moved out of orbit, but they somehow find a way back to that orbit, forever changed from the collision. Antonio forever changed you, and he is a part of who you are today. You will find your way back to your orbit. Have faith." He looked to see tears silently sliding down Aurora's cheeks.

"Thank you," Aurora reached across the counter and touched his hand. Nick took the moment to pass the word *forgiveness* to her. Perhaps if she could forgive herself for not attending the funeral she would be able to make advances in her healing. "I need to go prepare for a tour. I'm glad I met you. Sorry again for yelling at you." She smiled shyly as she wiped at her cheeks and then pulled on her coat. "Ciao, Nick." He waved as she left the café. The sound of the bells on the door handle signaled the end of their own cosmic collision.

CHAPTER 25

Nick again knocked at A. Fortini 26. He heard Beatrice's light footsteps and once again was greeted by her disgruntled frown. He held up his plastic pastry container with a hopeful smile. She looked at the offering and her shoulders fell in amused defeat, the corners of her mouth lifting slightly as she shook her head and took the raspberry éclair. She gave him the feelings of a misbehaving student bringing an apple to the teacher - someone recently forgiven, that should tread carefully.

"He's back in his office. I hope you brought the book. He's mentioned it about twenty-three times." She gestured toward the office and stood aside.

"Thank you, Mrs. Wilhelmus," Nick said as he walked down the familiar hallway. He knocked lightly as he opened the office door. Daniel didn't look up, just raised his pointer finger while he finished what he was reading. He then dropped his hand, closed his book, and looked up.

"Ah, Nick, you're here. Wonderful." Daniel stood and removed his glasses. He set them down and waved his hand for Nick to join him behind the desk. "Bring that chair around, would you? I have a lot to show you." Nick leaned his staff against the wall next to the door before grabbing the chair. He squeezed it behind the desk and had just enough room to fit his legs uncomfortably against the desks drawers as he sat down. Daniel moved the reading lamp on his desk so it would shine between the two of them and then shuffled the copied page of the book over to Nick, along with his notes. "Where to begin…" Daniel mumbled to himself. Nick didn't care as long as he started receiving answers. His musing last night about Ben's odd behavior left him feeling unsettled and impatient to return to the Time Room. Hopefully, he'd find at least a note from his elusive friend.

"This text differs slightly from what I've seen in my studies throughout the years. Do you have the book with you?" he asked eagerly. Nick pressed his cloak aside to reach into his bag. He pulled the book out and set it next to the copied page.

"Excellent. I just wanted to cross reference a few of the symbols with others in the book to see if my translations are as correct as they can be." Daniel's finger flipped gently through the book until he landed on a page of writing that seemed to satisfy his curiosity. He looked between the page and his copy, then to his notes, and back again. He would put on his glasses and remove them every half minute. Nick doubted Daniel even realized he was doing it. He sat still while this continued for another twenty minutes. Ready for answers, Nick cleared his throat. Daniel jumped and turned to him as if he'd appeared out of thin air.

"Oh yes, sorry. This is all so fascinating. Look here, these symbols all match with the one here," he pointed to the symbols on the printed page. "I've used what I know of Egyptian hieroglyphics and other written languages to make my best guess at what these words mean, and now, after looking here," he pointed to several symbols in the book. "I believe my translations to be correct." Daniel sat back and placed his glasses on top of his head, rubbing at his eyes. If what Mrs. Wilhelmus said was true, then he must be exhausted. Nick shifted further back in his seat, trying to give his knees a reprieve from being smashed into the desk. Daniel took Nick's movement as impatience, which perhaps was not unfounded. He set the copied page on top of the open book and pulled a pen from behind his ear.

"This top line here," Daniel pointed, "is hard to read, especially these first few words, because of the fading, but the rest of the sentence refers to the map leading to a cave." Nick sat up straighter, ignoring the scraping pain in his knees, and leaned over the document. A cave? That couldn't be a coincidence. Daniel looked surprised by Nick's sudden shift and the atmosphere of the room changed. Nick could feel that Daniel was just as eager to tell him as Nick was to hear more.

"The second line," Daniel continued. "Granted, this is a rough translation, since the order of the words is different in most ancient texts. It says something like 'Time continues, he remains unseen, trapped in his... despair', perhaps ... the last line has the most easily recognizable symbol in it." Daniel pointed to the last word on the page.

"And what is that?" Nick asked, his mouth going dry. The symbol looked like some sort of beetle or scorpion to him.

"Traitor." Nick could sense Daniel's pleasure at having known the translation, but it changed to concern when he saw the color draining from Nick's face.

"Are you alright, Nick? Should I call Beatrice to bring some water?" Daniel asked quickly, taking his glasses from his head and placing them next to the book on the counter. Nick quickly composed himself, at least outwardly.

"No, just surprised. It's all very... exciting." He cleared his throat after the last word came out in a rasp. "What does the rest of the line say?"

"That is the trickiest part. It's written like a prophecy or perhaps a warning, as if the writer is telling the reader that taking the map will count them as a traitor and lead them to their own moral destruction. There is also mention of a beast, but that could be symbolic of a lot of other things." Nick sat back in his chair, the shift causing a new ache in his knees. His hand went to his face as Daniel continued enthusiastically.

"Such an exciting find. I know you can't tell me where you found it, but this one will stay with me, I am sure." Daniel's knee bounced. "A writing like this so ancient and prophetic is the dream of scholars like myself and our mutual friend Allie."

Daniel continued, but Nick was not listening. A traitor. Someone breaking the seal, stealing the map. A map to a cave that held a powerful mystical beast. One with red, glowing eyes. That wasn't in the text, but Nick remembered clearly. If Daniel's translation was correct, which he felt confident it was, then someone was searching for the Shadow's cave. Nick turned and stood. He gathered the book and the copy he'd left with Daniel, quickly placing them into his bag and moving around the desk to grab his staff. The warmth that radiated into him from the staff was comforting, as usual, but not enough to dispel his building anxiety. He needed to return to the Time Room. Now.

"Sir? Nick? Wait. Are you leaving? I'd love to study more of the book. We could work together."

"You have been most helpful, but I'm afraid I must go. I have your payment." He shuffled around in his bag and withdrew a respectable stack of euro.

"As a retired college professor, I won't turn down the money. Though it was a pleasure to be presented with such a challenge. It was nice to put my mind to work again." He chuckled. Nick thanked him and opened the door to the office. He was halfway to the front door when he heard Mrs. Wilhelmus clattering around in the kitchen. He spun around and returned to the office, his footsteps muffled along the long Persian rug.

Daniel had settled into the office chair again, his hands clasped over his stomach, and was rocking slowly back and forth, looking absentmindedly at the wall. Nick watched him for a moment before knocking on the open door to draw Daniel's attention.

"Have you forgotten something?" he asked, coming to his feet.

"No, no, well, just this." Nick extended a hand out to Daniel and looked him directly in the eye. He channeled his power into the handshake and transferred the word *content*. Daniel deserved peace of mind in his retirement. Knowledge that his academic and professional work was complete and he could move on to the next phase in his life. He hoped he would take that word and not idle away his time, but realize that he could leave all his past projects in their rightful place and pass them along to the next generation. Only time would tell. He said another farewell and headed back to the hallway, leaving Daniel standing in wonder at the mysterious man that had passed in and out of his life so swiftly. As Nick reached the door, Mrs. Wilhelmus came from the kitchen, wiping her hands on her apron. He bowed respectfully, then saw himself out.

CHAPTER 26

Nick rushed through the Rome library and into the Time Room. He placed his hands on the railing that circled the globe to steady himself. Forcing himself to take a few deep breaths, he shut his eyes. He'd never had a panic attack, and had only experienced it through others. He wasn't eager to have the experience himself.

The journey back to the Time Room had seemed excruciatingly slow. Feeling his heart rate slow and the throbbing in his head weaken, he walked to the council room to look at Allie's board. No note. He headed back into the Rome library. It was late and the library would close soon. He headed to Allie's office hoping she was working late. As he approached the door, he was relieved to see a light shining through the semitransparent window in the door. As he lifted his hand to knock, the door opened, and a man ran directly into him. The man might've been handsome, with his dark hair and strong stature, but it was hard to see past the man's puffy red eyes and runny nose. The man let out a loud sneeze that echoed off the walls of the quiet library before looking at Nick.

"Permesso," the man mumbled, stepping around Nick and heading quickly toward the entrance of the library. Nick caught the door before it closed and stepped inside. Allie was leaning with her hands on either side of her head, two fingers messaging the space between her hairline and eyebrows. Cha-cha was cuddled in her lap.

"Are you making grown men cry now?" Nick said. He couldn't pass up the opportunity to tease, despite his rush. Allie looked up in surprise.

"You know full well that man wasn't sad," she said to Nick with a glare. Nick silently agreed. There had been nothing but arrogance coming from that man.

"Have you heard from Ben?" Nick asked.

"No, but I haven't checked the board today..." she said wearily.

"I just came from there," Nick said, cutting her off. "There's nothing." He paused tapping his fingers on his staff. "I'm going to his cabin."

"Would you like me to come? I have a few things here that need to be done, but I can clear my schedule tomorrow morning."

"No, I'll make this trip alone. I'm leaving now. It's a day's walk once out of the Auckland library. I just need to check in and make sure everything is okay." He left out the part where he didn't think she would be a great audience when he subtly asked Ben if he had betrayed them.

"Was Daniel able to translate the book? You weren't gone for as long as I thought."

"He was, and he made quick work of it."

"What did it say?" she asked slowly.

"I'm not ready to share that yet, and I need to see Ben. I'm sorry I can't give a better answer, but it will all come out in time."

"Time," she scoffed. "That's one thing we have in spades. I've grown enough patience over the years to wait."

"Thank you for understanding." With a quick turn, Nick made his second hasty exit of the day.

***

Nick's senses were inundated with the spice of the evergreen trees on either side of the winding path covered in fallen pine needles. He took in the scent of the evergreen trees surrounding him. A rabbit leapt off the path in front of him and into a bush. Above him, a crow cawed, an owl hooted, and the wind rustled the trees. The light rays streaming through the tops of the trees did little for the cold pricking at his exposed skin. The light faded as he walked, and he knew he wouldn't make it before darkness completely fell. When it became too dark to continue, he stepped away from the path and used his bag as a pillow. He lay down, then moved some pinecones out from under his back. He would be comfortable enough to wait out the night. As he tucked his cloak tightly around him, his thoughts turned to tomorrow's confrontation. Ben had always been steady, always willing to follow the call of the Creator. Nick had always admired that. Nick rarely experienced frustration with being unable to read the emotions of his fellow protectors, but in this moment, he was. He might have been able to diffuse his eruption at Kaida before it had even begun. He could have been able to tell what was behind his discomfort beyond just being claustrophobic indoors. Was Ben a traitor? That was the question behind all the others. What reason would Ben have for betraying them, or the Creator? Was there a lead up, an event, a secret? Nick shoved aside the questions and tried to clear his mind, to allow for some answers to come to him from the Creator, but nothing came. He would have to wait until morning, and hope that Ben was at his cottage to answer.

***

Nick stood as soon as the sun broke over the horizon enough to see. He'd have to walk most of the day to get to Ben. His feet occasionally slid across the wet needles strewn across the path but he trudged on, covering the miles of ground that kept Ben's cottage well-hidden and secluded from the rest of the world.

He'd left the main path and knew he was getting close as the sun set. He heard movement ahead of him and looked to the ground to see what creature was causing the stir. His eyes fell on a well-worn pair of brown boots encircled by a green cloak. His gaze continued upward until they met the dark eyes of his friend. A friendship he'd never doubted before his trip to Assisi. Naturally, one of the forest animals would have alerted Ben of his approach.

Ben's green cloak swung to a stop as he planted his feet and looked at Nick. Ben held his staff across his body. His stance was firm and defensive.

"What are you doing here, Nick?" Ben asked angrily.

"What have you done, Ben?" Nick blurted, imitating Ben's stance. So much for a subtle approach. A hawk cawed and landed on Ben's shoulder, its head turned with one black eye looking unblinkingly at Nick. A rabbit bounded out of a bush and stopped at Ben's feet.

"I have done nothing," Ben said dismissively. His gaze was steady on Nick's face. His eyebrows lowered.

"You missed the meeting," Nick said.

"Is that why you're here? To ask why I didn't attend the meeting?" His eye sparked with a challenge as he took a half step back and leaned forward. Nick took a steadying breath. His pulse throbbed in his hand from the tight grip he held on his staff. They'd sparred before and Nick knew that Ben was the superior fighter.

"Can we go to your cottage and discuss this?"

"No," Ben said definitively. Nick stepped back. In the centuries of knowing Ben, he had never been harsh. He'd always welcomed any of the protectors to his home.

"Ben, what is this? Why such a cold greeting?" For the first time, Ben faltered. His eyes shifted to the side and then snapped back to Nick. "What are you hiding?" Nick pressed, fearing the answer.

"This doesn't concern you, Nick."

"Ben, please. Whatever this is, we can fix it. We can find the will of the Creator. The Shadow is our common enemy, Ben. Do not turn your back on us now." Ben's arm dropped to his side and his stance straightened. He turned his back to Nick, walked a few steps away, and then spun back to face him. His hawk squawked in protest, ruffling its feathers, but didn't fly off. Ben's birds' loyalty was faultless and intimidating. Ben ran a hand over the top of his short black hair and let out a frustrated growl. Nick's hand loosened on his staff and he took two steps toward Ben.

"The Shadow? Is that why you're here? You think I..." Ben rubbed his forehead and glanced into the tops of the trees, cursing under his breath. "Come with me." Ben grabbed his staff and Nick followed, unsure what caused the sudden change in Ben's demeanor. Despite his suspicions, he followed him, trusting what he felt he knew about Ben's character.

They walked further down the less traveled path and as they came to a small bridge crossing a stream, Ben's cottage came into view. The cottage was not as close as Nick had thought. He also didn't remember there being a bridge to cross. Then a wave of giggly excitement washed over him, not his own. He didn't think he himself had experienced this emotion ever in his life.

"Ben..." Nick began cautiously.

"Just come on. I knew this day would come eventually," Ben said resignedly.

CHAPTER 27

"Thank you, Fern," Ben said, as they came to the front door. Nick wanted to say something about Ben talking to plants when a large fox uncurled from the shadow of the front step, bowed its head slightly and stalked off into the trees.

"I'm ready for answers." Nick said, watching the fox disappear into the surrounding forest. Ben looked at Nick, opened his mouth, then closed it.

"It's just been the two of us, I just... she hasn't... I... okay." Ben swung open the door and stood aside. Nick stooped down slightly so he could enter, then rose to his full height once inside. The cottage had a living space, a kitchen to the left and a bedroom to the right. A fire roared next to the reclining chair. Nick noticed the additions since the last time he'd been there. The bookshelf was the same, but the contents contained younger literature -fairy tales and picture books. There was a smaller chair matching the big recliner. There was a wooden dollhouse in one corner with doll clothes and accessories scattered about. The open door to the bedroom showed a small bed on the wall opposite Ben's. Peeking around the doorway was a little girl. She had large blue eyes, blonde hair to her waist, and a nightgown. The same nervous excitement he'd sensed as they approached filled him again as her eyes met his.

"Come here, dearest," Ben said, coming to one knee and opening his arms. The girl ran into his embrace. Nick was speechless. Ben picked up the girl and turned to Nick, balancing her on his hip. "Nick, I'd like you to meet Rayne. My daughter. Rayne, this is Daddy's friend Nick. Can you say hi?" Rayne lifted her hand and waved before turning her head into Ben's shoulder shyly. Nick thought she looked to be about five or six years old. Ben squeezed her tight. Nick just stared. "Now, I believe before I left, I had tucked you into bed. Am I remembering right, or am I getting old?" Ben said as Rayne giggled.

"Definitely old, Daddy. Can I stay up with you?" she looked up with big round eyes and an eager smile. Nick had the feeling this little girl usually got her way. He'd sure have a hard time saying no to that little face.

"I need to visit with my friend. Why don't we get you some water and then tuck you back into bed?" Ben said. Rayne exhaled loudly.

"And a cookie," she negotiated. Nick chuckled at her tactics and the image of Ben baking cookies.

"You've already brushed your teeth. You can have one tomorrow." Ben turned to Nick. "Have a seat while I get this one back to bed."

"It was a pleasure to meet you, Miss Rayne." Nick said with a bow, causing her to giggle again. He sat in the recliner as Ben went to the kitchen to get his daughter some water. Daughter. His uneasiness at the meeting and eagerness to leave. Where had she been? Surely, he hadn't left her with a fox that whole time? A daughter. She looked nothing like Ben. Nick's head swirled with questions, but stopped when Ben tucked his daughter into bed.

"Will you tell me a story?" he heard her ask from the bedroom.

"Very well," Ben said with the exhale of an exhausted parent. He told a story of two birds that hatched an egg. The birds then took off on a journey and could not return. The baby bird was alone and afraid when along came a wise owl. "Where did you come from, little one? The wise owl asked." Ben gave the owl an overly deep voice. "The bird was too young to answer the wise old owl, but the owl knew the bird needed help. So he scooped her up and carried her home, where the wise old owl took care of the bird for the rest of her days. She never went without food or love or anything. The end. Goodnight, little bird."

"Goodnight, Daddy." The love and pure goodness that came from the girl caused Nick's throat to tighten. Children like her were all that was right in this world. Ben came from the room and closed the door behind him. He walked to the kitchen and brought a wooden chair into the sitting room. He placed it facing the fire at the same angle as Nick's and took a seat. They sat in silence for a while. Nick hoped Ben would speak first and voluntarily answer some of his questions. When the silence continued, he finally asked.

"Does the wise owl know what happened to the little bird's parents?" There was another stretch of silence.

"Yes," was Ben's soft answer. Nick observed Ben's face and saw a war of emotions. They fell into silence again and Nick didn't press. He sat watching the flames and listening to the cackling of the fire.

"How did she come into your care?" Nick asked.

"I found her as a baby, here in this forest. I'm all she can remember."

"She must be five?"

"I believe six. We celebrate her birthday on the first day of spring each year, but of course I don't know her actual birthday." Nick wanted to ask a thousand more questions, but looked at Ben's guarded expression and thought better. Ben was a wise owl. There was nothing that Nick could ask that Ben wouldn't already have considered, but one thought still nagged at him.

"You know she will grow old. You will watch her return to the Creator. She will realize at some point that you do not age."

"Yes," Ben answered. "Her life is worth it. She wouldn't be here if I hadn't found her. Her life will be unconventional, but I will love and care for her. I saved her from perhaps the end the Creator prepared for her, though I believe it was Him that led me to her. I will not waste her second chance. She's beautiful, brave and smart. No mortal that has ever walked this earth will know more about this world, nature, and the animals than she does. Rayne is already my everything." Nick's heart burned at Ben's sincerity.

"Okay," Nick said.

"That's all?" Ben asked, astonished.

"What did you expect?" Nick asked, taken aback.

"A protest, a million questions, a... something," Ben's voice trailed off. Nick stood and leaned against the fireplace mantle, watching the flickering of the fire as it burned at the large oak log.

"You understand the depth of your responsibility to the people of this earth. You understand the expectations of the Creator. I will not question your judgment on this matter." He turned to face Ben. "I just wonder why you said nothing five years ago." Ben chuckled underneath his breath and leaned his elbows forward onto his knees.

"I guess I underestimated your understanding. I've meditated on this for countless hours and have never felt the Creator's disapproval. Part of me was overwhelmed by the idea of single parenthood, especially those first few months. The animals have helped. Their instinct in parenthood is inspirational, but this is unlike anything I've done before."

"I'd imagine not." Nick smiled. "I'm happy for you. Happy for me as well. I couldn't reconcile your behavior at this last council meeting with your character. It wasn't right- your behavior, your eagerness to leave. It was because of Rayne."

"Yes. I have so much more to lose now. It's not just about me anymore. The idea of raising Rayne in a time of war terrifies me. That fear turned to anger, and I lashed out. I will find time to apologize to Kaida again. When I heard the voice of the Shadow, my instinct was to return to Rayne as soon as possible and make sure she was okay. Despite seeing her reading a book with our librarian friend, I took her and returned here as quickly as possible. This feels like the safest place to me."

"That makes sense," Nick said. "I wouldn't worry too much about Kaida. Politics gives you tough skin, but I'm sure the gesture would be appreciated."

"Yes," Ben agreed. "Now, a question for you, my old friend." His eyes became dark as he looked directly into Nick's eyes. "Why did you assume that my not attending the meeting last week was a sign I was involved with the Shadow?"

Nick pushed off the mantle and returned to the recliner. He turned to Ben in the wooden dining room seat. "Do you want to switch chairs? This could take a while."

CHAPTER 28

Ben sat staring into the fire, deep in thought. The night had passed around them as they went back and forth on the meaning of the translation Nick had received from Daniel. The urgency in the air pulsed and waned as they went in circles on the likeliness of the cave being discovered. Nick turned away from the fire and saw the tight grip Ben had on the arm of his chair, his other hand rubbing at the dark stubble on his chin.

"A traitor," Ben whispered. "Who? I can't imagine any of us betraying the rest. It's been centuries of working together for the good of the people of the earth. Why would someone turn their back on the Creator? Why would anyone wish to help that vile creature?" They had cycled through these questions for hours, never with a suitable answer and always attached to more questions.

"Now that I no longer believe it's you…" Nick said, and Ben sent him a disapproving glare, "I don't know. I agree, it's hard to imagine. So, do we believe in the prophecy or warning or whatever you'd like to call it, or not? Just the fact that someone broke the seal of the forbidden books makes me question the integrity of the protectors. It's unheard of. Why now, after all these years? I fear I have many more questions than answers."

"As do I," Ben agreed solemnly. A small shuffling of feet came from the bedroom and Nick glanced to the window. The morning light streamed around the edges of the curtains. He looked back as Rayne came running to sit in Ben's lap.

"Good morning! How did you sleep?" Ben asked Rayne enthusiastically.

"Very well. I had incredible dreams." She settled her head back against Ben's chest and he rocked them for a few moments before Rayne sat up and turned to look at Ben's face. "Daddy, what's a traitor?" Ben looked at Nick with raised eyebrows. Someone had been eavesdropping.

"That is a significant question. Where did you hear that word?" Rayne looked up bashfully and shrugged. "A traitor is someone that was deeply trusted by another person and then they betray that trust."

"Like when a raccoon pretends to be friendly with another animal only to snatch its food and run away?" Nick wasn't surprised that Rayne used an animal reference for clarification, considering who her adoptive father was.

"That could be seen as treacherous behavior, especially to the animal that had its food snatched." Ben said. He squeezed Rayne tight and tickled her sides until she squealed and wiggled to the floor.

"I need to run to the forest. I'll be quick. Is Nick staying for breakfast?" Rayne asked.

"Only if he likes acai berry juice and whole grain chia seed pancakes!"

"Sounds amazing," Nick agreed, rubbing his stomach dramatically for Rayne's amusement. She smiled and headed to the door and slipped on a pair of bright yellow rain boots. She stood on her toes to get her small blue raincoat from off the coat rack.

"Take a hawk with you," Ben said as Rayne opened the door. Rayne whistled two high notes, and a hawk landed on her shoulder.

"That's an impressive whistle for a six-year-old," Nick said, amused. "and her vocabulary, not that of a typical six-year-old, I'd say."

"When it's just the two of us out here, there is a lot of time to learn little life skills, and with me being the only one to talk to aside from the animals, I guess she's picked up a lot of my words." Ben paused and stared at the door after his daughter left. Nick saw his expression go from admiration to determination. "I'm coming with you."

"Where?" Nick asked, perplexed.

"To the cave," Ben answered. There was silence as they both accepted the next step in finding answers.

"Who will stay with Rayne? Surely, you can't leave her with Fern for two weeks. It could be longer."

Ben turned back to the fire, now reduced to a few glowing embers. As Nick watched him, the corners of Ben's mouth slowly lifted.

"I know who can watch her," he said. Those were the only words of explanation and yet Nick had a strong feeling he knew exactly who the babysitter would be.

CHAPTER 29

The journey back to the Time Room seemed faster and slower. Faster with Ben and Rayne's company, slower because they went at the pace of a six-year-old. As soon as Rayne had her fill of pancakes, they'd packed her and Ben each a bag and headed into the forest. It took a few miles for Nick to get used to the slower pace and the sounds of the animals all around them.

"Is this normal when you travel?" Nick asked, looking over at Ben, who had scooped Rayne up and was giving her a ride on his back.

"Me carrying her? Yeah, it was easier when she was smaller and I had a hiking backpack to put her in." Nick loved that mental image. How had Ben kept such a big secret?

"No, I mean the animals," Nick said, gesturing to the small flock of various types of birds soaring closely over their heads and the woodland creatures running around their feet. Nick had traveled to and from Ben's cottage multiple times, but never with him.

"They don't follow you when you come to my cottage?" Ben asked.

"The only animal movement I see is when they startle and fly or scurry off the path to get away from me." Ben's astonished look caused Nick to laugh.

"I suppose that makes sense. I am their greatest ally, after all."

"Can I ride on Nick's back?" Rayne asked sleepily.

"Am I not going fast enough for you?" Ben asked jokingly, sprinting for a few yards, causing Rayne to giggle and grip his neck tighter. Nick sprinted to catch up.

"If I were Jack, this would become a race," Nick regaled. "I, however, prefer a steady pace. Rayne, come here." In one smooth motion, he'd gathered the girl from Ben's back and placed her securely on his own. Ben rolled his shoulders, looking grateful for the reprieve. They were stronger than mortals, but even protectors had their limits.

Nick felt the pressure and gentle bounce of the girl on his back. He stumbled slightly when a forest mouse ran across the path almost directly beneath his foot. Rayne tightened her arms.

"I won't drop you. I promise," Nick said, turning his head. From the corner of his eye, he could see that her eyes were closed.

"I know," she said with a yawn. Nick felt humbled. The ability of this child to trust a man she had just met because her father deemed him safe was incredible. Her innocence reminded him of the goodness of this world, the hope there was for the future. The weight of her on his back was nothing compared to the weight of helping this world become a better place for her to live in. Ben had taken on an enormous task. Rayne's weight shifted, and her head fell onto his shoulder. Her breathing slowed, and she was soon asleep.

"Do you want me to take her?" Ben asked quietly, after they'd walked a few more miles.

"No, I'm fine. Let her rest," he whispered. "You are doing well, Ben. She is so content, trusting and honest. I can feel it all."

"I worry the world will knock that out of her. Her goodness and optimism. I want to protect it," Ben said with a sad smile. Nick had no answer. If everyone could keep the innocence of their youth, the world would be a better, more creative, wholesome place. They continued walking another hour; in that time Rayne woke up and walked between them chattering like the squirrels that ran across the path and jumped from the trees above them. She asked Ben questions about almost every plant or animal she saw. He answered every question with great detail. Nick pulled out the sandwiches and trail mix they'd prepared at the cottage and they ate as they walked. A few hours later, darkness had fallen.

"We are only a few hours away from the library, but it'll be closed, and I don't think we should keep going in the dark. It looks like someone is getting tired again," Ben said, noticing Rayne's yawn. "If we rest until the sun rises, then we should arrive just as the library is opening."

"Sounds perfect. How do you feel about sleeping outside, Rayne?" Nick said, looking down at her.

"We sleep outside all the time!" Rayne said, bouncing on her toes. "How else would we learn the stars?" she said, as if it were obvious.

Nick and Ben would have their cloaks to keep them warm, and Ben pulled a blanket out of his bag for Rayne. They found a spot off the path that was clear of rocks and settled down. Ben and Nick used their bags as pillows, and Rayne used Ben's arm. Ben quizzed Rayne on the few constellations they could see through the tops of the trees until she fell asleep. Nick had not rested since his night in Assisi and he'd made the journey between Ben's cottage almost twice. It didn't take long for him to drift off to sleep.

In the morning, they had more trail mix for breakfast as they walked the rest of the way to the Auckland library. They hadn't made it three steps into the library before a voice echoed through the library.

"Rayne! Is that you? Look at how you've grown!"

"Mimi!" Rayne exclaimed, releasing Ben's hand to greet her friend. The woman was old and robust. Her white hair and wrinkles made her look like a classic painting of a Mrs. Claus. Nick smirked at the thought and then raised his eyebrows at Ben. He looked about to explain when the woman called out again.

"Ben, get over here and introduce your friend." Ben smiled at Nick and waved him forward.

"Hello, Gertrude," Ben said, giving her a kiss on the cheek. "This is my friend, Nick. He traveled with us today."

"It's so good to meet you!" she said, standing and wrapping Nick in a hug, pinning his arms to his sides.

"You as well. Is it Gertrude or Mimi?"

"All the children that come in call me Mimi," she said. "It's easier to say than Gertrude. Prettier too. Whichever you prefer!" she said with a warm smile. She squeezed Rayne's hand and bent down to be closer.

"Why don't you and I go look at some books in the children's section?"

"Not today!" Ben stepped in. "We need to go meet up with another friend." Rayne looked up at Ben with giant eyes.

"Just a few new books? I'll pick really fast!" she pleaded. Ben's face showed conflicting emotions. He finally turned to Nick.

"Do we have a moment?" he asked.

"For books? Always," Nick said, smiling at Rayne. She skipped off, holding Gertrude's hand, talking a mile a minute about their trip to the library – their trek through the forest, getting a piggyback ride, the animals running all around them.

"Such a big adventure," Gertrude said, clearly thinking Rayne was just making up stories. It did sound pretty fantastical coming from a six-year-old.

When Rayne's arms were full of new books, they said their goodbyes to Gertrude and snuck around the back shelf of the library and disappeared into the Time Room.

Rayne looked around, eyes as big as saucers. She approached the railing that surrounded the golden globe and dropped her library books to the ground. She climbed the bottom rung so she could see better. As she reached out a hand to touch it, Ben grabbed her hand and lifted her gently back to the ground. He got on one knee to look her in the eyes. He lay his staff on the ground beside him and held Rayne's shoulders.

"Rayne. Do you remember when you asked me why the animals come to me and why I talk to them when they can't talk back?"

"You mean when you told me you can understand them and I'm not supposed to tell anyone?"

"Yes," Ben chuckled. "To put it simply. This room is like my talking with the animals. It's special. Something just for our family and we don't talk about it with others. Do you understand?" She nodded her head and then her eyes lit up.

"Does that mean Nick is part of my family?" Her eyes glowed as she looked over at Nick. Ben looked at Nick, looking unsure how to answer. Nick came over and knelt down beside Ben.

"Definitely," Nick said, and Rayne flung her arms around his neck. "Oh, ho, ho." Nick laughed as he caught his balance and returned the hug. "If you think this is great, wait until you meet your dad's other friends." He took Rayne's hand and stood. He looked at Ben and saw a look of gratitude. What else were the protectors to each other if not family?

They walked together toward the door to the Rome library and entered. Nick took a moment to orient himself. Rome and New Zealand were a twelve-hour time difference. While the day was beginning where they'd left, here the day was just ending.

"Does this library have a children's section?" Rayne asked, her voice filled with wonder. She looked up at the bookshelves that were floor to ceiling, her eyes wide and mouth hanging ajar.

"I'm not sure, but I know who you can ask," Nick said, gently tugging her hand to get her moving again. After checking Allie's office, and not finding her there, the next place to look was her apartment. They walked around the long tables and the three of them stepped out into the streets of Rome. The air was chilly and Ben stopped to zip up Rayne's coat.

"Do you need a hat?" he asked. Rayne shook her head, seeming impatient.

"Allie said her apartment was under construction and that she'd moved to the one across the street." Ben said, turning to Nick. "Have you been to the new one?"

"No, just her office."

The construction of Allie's old apartment was obvious and well underway by the looks of it. Before they turned the corner onto the street, they heard the sounds of tractors, lifts, and workers. Orange cones and piles of construction material surrounded the building. It didn't look as if she'd be returning to her beloved ancient architecture apartment for some time.

Directly across the street was another apartment building, much newer, the windows covered in a layer of dust from the construction work across the street. Nick and Ben exchanged a look before heading to the building.

"Any guesses which number she lives at?" Ben asked as they climbed a set of metal stairs. Nick had one trick up his sleeve. He stopped halfway up the stairs and reached out to the feelings of everyone around him. The entire spectrum of emotions could be felt as they passed each door. He continued up the stairs, feeling each room they passed until he reached one that he couldn't feel anything from. He knocked on the door, but there was no answer, so they continued on. The next time he couldn't feel any emotions from behind an apartment door, was on the third floor, about halfway down the hallway. There was a wreath on the door that was made entirely of pages from old books. Someone had cut and folded the pages to resemble fresh flowers and swirls. This was definitely the place. Nick raised his hand and knocked. There was a shuffle inside and the sound of a book hitting the floor. The door opened an inch, stopped by a metal lock at the top of the door.

"Nick! Hi!" Allie greeted, closing the door, unlocking, and re-opening it. Her hair was wound up and secured in a clip on the back of her head and Nick could see slippers poking out from under her ivory robe.

"And Ben!" her eyes lit up with joy then relief as they entered. "We missed you at council. I was so worried. Wait, who's this?" Allie said, as Rayne peeked out shyly from behind Ben's leg. Ben took a deep breath and looked down at Rayne.

"Allie, I'd like you to meet Rayne. My daughter." A thick silence filled the room as if everyone were holding their breath. Then a loud squeal echoed off the small apartment walls.

"I'm an aunt!" Allie all but shouted. She dropped to her knees in front of Rayne and held out her arms. Rayne didn't even hesitate before launching herself into Allie's embrace. If Nick looked surprised, it was nothing to the look of shock on Ben's face. Allie held Rayne at arm's length. "I'm Allie. Rayne, what a beautiful name, so fitting. Let me take your coat, tell me how old you are. Oh wait, are you hungry? I'll make cookies!"

"Can I help?" Rayne asked, seeming unphased by Allie's exuberance.

"Absolutely, sweetheart. I want to hear all about you. This might be the best day of my life." She took Rayne's coat and tossed it onto the couch. She took the small girl's hand, and they walked to the kitchen together, leaving Ben and Nick in the living room staring after them.

"What just happened?" Ben asked slowly. His expression made Nick laugh.

"I think you just made Allie's dreams come true. Come on, we'd better watch and make sure Allie doesn't let her eat all the cookie dough."

CHAPTER 30

The scene in the kitchen was endearing. Rayne tried to tie Allie's apron around her back and Allie pulled ingredients out of the cupboard and threw them down on the counter.

"I have the best recipe for cookies from the 1800s. It's a classic. I do like to add a little extra sugar, though. It's not as scarce as it was back then."

"I'll get the recipe book!" Rayne exclaimed, turning in a circle, searching for where it might be. Allie chuckled, and Rayne looked confused. She glanced at Ben, who explained as he tied the apron securely behind her back.

"You know my gift with animals." Rayne nodded. "Allie remembers everything. Anything she's seen or read. She has many college degrees and is a brilliant historian."

"Oh, stop it," Allie said, blushing. Ben did, but only because Cha-cha came flying out of nowhere into Ben's arms.

"Well, hello there!" Ben laughed, cuddling the cat into his chest and stroking its fur.

"You have a cat!" Rayne's little voice caused the cat's head to turn.

"That's Cha-cha," Allie introduced. "I've had her since she was a tiny little kitten," Allie said to Rayne. The little girl, already enraptured by her new-found aunt, now liked her even more.

"She doesn't like the new brand of cat food you switched to." Ben added matter-of-factly. Allie stared hard at her cat, one eyebrow raised, before smiling.

"Well, Princess Cha-cha, why didn't you say so? We'll switch back." Ben must have relayed the message because a soft purring rumbled deep within the cat.

"Ok, everything is ready. Are you ready to start measuring? You boys go find something else to do. You're welcome to sit in the living room. It's probably the most comfortable."

Nick smiled at their dismissal and could hear the beeping of the oven as Allie showed Rayne how to preheat it. The two of them settled into the living room. A copy of Pride and Prejudice lay on the floor. Nick wondered if Jane Austen was one of the many author friends Allie had made over the centuries. He'd have to ask another time. Ben settled into the chair in the corner, Cha-cha settled into his lap. He had a feeling the cat wouldn't leave Ben until forced to. The animals loved him. Ben had his gaze fixed on the cat as he slowly stroked her fur. Nick rested his eyes and looked forward to the cookies the girls were making. Every time Ben said, "hmmm," Nick's ear would twitch, but he knew Ben wasn't directing it at him. Ben was having a conversation with a house cat. Nick wondered passively what a cat would have to say. He could hear the girls talking and giggling from the small apartment kitchen as well. His mind was at peace until it wandered again to the journey Ben and Nick were about to embark on. His stomach twisted with nerves, but he pushed those away as best he could. They'd prepare before leaving. It was the best they could do.

A few minutes later, the girls joined them in the living room. Allie settled on the other end of the couch that Nick was on and Rayne climbed into Ben's lap, adjusting Cha-cha so she could pet her soft belly.

"Is someone bothering you Allie?" Ben blurted.

"Excuse me?" Allie said in surprise.

"Cha-cha says that she comes to work with you because someone is bothering you."

"Oh," she laughs, "she must mean Jack. Those two never seem to get along." She gave Cha-cha a pointed look, and the cat jumped off Ben's lap and headed to another part of the apartment. Ben didn't look completely convinced, but let it drop. Nick remembered the man that ran into him coming out of Allie's office a few days ago but decided to follow Ben's lead.

The oven timer beeped, and Allie left to pull the cookies from the oven.

"What do you think of Allie?" Ben asks Rayne.

"I love her. Is she really my aunt? Another part of our family?"

"She's as close to me as any sister would be, I suppose. How would you like to stay with her for a few days?"

"Can I?" she asked, bouncing on her knees in Ben's lap. "We'd have so much fun. She said she could show me the children's section at the library, and there's a park not too far away." Nick smiled again. Allie hadn't missed a beat. She knew exactly what she wanted to do with her newly found niece. "Where are you going, Daddy?"

"Nick and I are going to take a trip into the mountains."

"Which mountains?" Allie asked sharply. All eyes turned to see her standing in the entrance to the living room holding the much-anticipated plate of cookies. Her gaze burned into Nick and then darted to Ben and then to Rayne.

"The mountains where an ancient creature is being held bound." Ben answered Allie's question but kept his eyes on Rayne. "We need to make sure everyone is still safe." Allie set the plate of cookies on the glass table and lowered herself to the couch, sinking into the cushions, looking exhausted. Then, as if a bolt of lightning struck her, she sat up as straight as a board.

"You can't take Rayne with you. I'll watch her," Allie said emphatically. Ben's dark eyes danced.

"I was hoping you'd say that," he admitted.

"It's settled then. I don't particularly agree with this journey of yours. It's tempting fate, but I trust both of you. If you think this is best, then go. We will be just fine, won't we, Rayne?"

"Daddy will be safe! And I bet you're a much more fun babysitter than Fern. She just guards the door and ignores me, even if I bring her food."

"Fern?" Allie asked, tilting her head.

"A fox," Ben clarified. Allie shook her head in disbelief. Nick could only imagine the spoiling that was about to happen under Allie's watchful eye.

CHAPTER 31

Nick sat in the living room as Allie and Ben tucked Rayne into her makeshift bed on the couch in Allie's small office. Ben had spent the last half hour giving detailed instructions on how to care for Rayne. He pulled more vials and eyedroppers and bottles of herbs from his bag then seemed possible, explaining the different uses and when to give them to Rayne and how much. It was a good thing he only had to tell Allie once; he would have had to tell and retell Nick for hours with him taking copious notes and even then, he felt sure he'd still get it wrong.

Allie joined him a few minutes later and they could hear Ben singing an Italian lullaby, the slow speed and deep notes floating down the hall of the small apartment. Allie looked at Nick, but he pretended not to notice. He knew what she was going to say. From the corner of his eye, he saw her still staring. He let out a low growl and uncrossed his arms, turning to face her.

"Okay, let's hear it."

"The Shadow. You're going to look for the Shadow? As in, intentionally seek him out. Have you lost your mind? Do you know how dangerous this is?" She paused and Nick waited to see if she'd continue before speaking.

"Yes," he began, but he was too quick. Allie wasn't finished.

"Do you really? I've done a lot of study over the years. Every culture has some version of the Shadow – the boogeyman, Satan, Krampus, Demogorgon. The Shadow is the opposition to the Creator. And I don't mean opposition in the mortal human sense, where the greed and selfishness of the natural man conflicts with the Creator's plan for the eternal destiny of his children. No, no, I'm talking about a being almost as powerful as the Creator himself. A being with nothing but malice and hate in his heart. The destruction he spreads doesn't bring him joy; it's simply his purpose and for a being as dark as him, it's all he has. You know he can't be destroyed, only trapped, which is what he is. Finding him will do you no good." She launched to her feet and paced. Ben's song stopped, and he came to join them in the living room. He sat and watched Allie walk back and forth across the rug. She paused her pacing and turned to Ben. He raised a reassuring hand.

"I heard you, Allie. At least the gist of it. Please don't tell Rayne of these fears. The heaviness of our role as protectors is ours, not hers."

"I would never. I just feel like... like... like time itself is standing on the edge of a cliff. Everything feels delicate, like a simple push or even a gust of wind will cast everything to the depths of a never-ending fall, surrendering everyone and everything we hold most dear into endless darkness, confusion, and chaos." The room was silent for two breaths.

"That's why we must go," Ben said. "Today I introduced you to the second most important thing in my life. The first is our role as protectors. For centuries, we have been aware that the release of the Shadow is inevitable. We know he's coming. We all feel it. Your analogy is accurate. Nick and I want to be on the front lines of this fight. When the Shadow is released, we are going to see darkness on this earth worse than we've ever seen. We have to be prepared."

"How does finding the Shadow prepare us?" she asked, her lips pressed into a fine line.

"You, more than anyone, know the value of knowledge. I can't believe my discovery of this book..." Nick lifted the forbidden book from his bag, "was an accident. If the Creator hadn't wanted it read, there would have been more resistance. I feel as if he is giving us a chance, letting us know he believes we are ready for more. More knowledge. More understanding."

"Or maybe no one was meant to see it. We don't know who took it from the shelf or why they wanted the map. You can't just aimlessly wander in the woods hoping to stumble upon a place that you think might be where the Shadow is hidden. There isn't enough information to go off of."

"Tell her," Ben said. Nick looked at Ben sharply. "Tell her what you told me the other night." Allie crossed her arms, annoyed by the men's secrecy.

"I know where the Shadow is. We aren't just going searching aimlessly, we will go directly to him," Nick said. Again, silence filled the room.

"How? The map was removed." Allie finally asked.

"When the Shadow spoke in the council room, I was given a vision. A map. I can't explain. It's in my head – the journey, the landscape, the markers, the cave."

"This is a trap. It has to be. The Shadow wouldn't give up his location. It makes no sense. And why you? Why not everyone?" She grabbed her staff from its place in the corner and absentmindedly passed it from hand to hand as she spoke. She pressed it firmly into the rug and placed her forehead against the smooth wood. The engraving lit up and pulsed at her forehead. She took a few calming breaths with her eyes closed. "It doesn't matter why. I trust you two. Just promise me you'll be careful." Nick and Ben each nodded solemnly. "Alright, then, what do you need from me?"

"Do you have a computer? We need to book some flights."

"Where are you heading?" she asked.

"Southeast Asia."

CHAPTER 32

The flight to Thailand was the first leg of a long journey. They landed and walked to a bus station. The bus took them to a small-town bordering Nan.

Nick settled into the seat next to Ben on the bus. Ben scooted forward and leaned back, resting his head back on the seat, his eyes closed. Nick pulled a notebook and pencil from his bag and sketched. A few hours later, he nudged Ben awake.

"We get out here," he said. Ben followed silently. They stepped down off the bus and Ben turned to look at Nick.

"Where to from here?" Nick felt a pull toward the road. He took a deep breath before relaying the news to Ben.

"From here, we walk." Ben nodded and gestured for Nick to lead the way. After a few miles of farmland and fields, the dirt road led to a small town on the edge of a thick forest. They walked through the town, feeling as if every eye was on them. Women walking in the streets grabbed their children's hands and pulled them closer to themselves. Men left their rocking chairs to go back into their homes. What were these people afraid of? They obviously weren't used to strangers this far off the beaten path. The last store on the lonely street they walked appeared to be a grocery store. They entered and saw what served as a store and bar. There were a few men with drinks seated at the counter and on the other side of the small building a woman with two children picked out soaps and shampoos. Nick approached the man standing behind the counter. He appeared to be in his late sixties, with a stooped neck and bushy eyebrows. The man bowed his head in greeting, not smiling, as he cleaned a glass with a rag. Nick assumed he spoke Thai instead of English. Ben sat on one of the bar stools, and the man poured him a glass of clear liquid. Ben looked at it closely, then when the man looked away, ran his hand over the glass. It bubbled as if boiling for a few seconds, then settled. Ben took a sip.

"We need to find a path that begins with a tree that looks like this," Nick said as he pulled his notebook from his bag and showed the man a picture of a tree he'd sketched on the bus. The tree itself wasn't anything unusual, perhaps a Banyan tree. Its defining feature was a deep curve in its trunk, the shape of the letter C, that ended in a knot in the wood big enough to sit on. The first path began right next to the tree. Nick's drawing skills were nothing inspiring, but as he showed it to the man, his eyebrows raised in recognition. Still, he said nothing.

"Can someone take us here?" Nick said pointing between himself and Ben, then to the tree sketch. "We can pay."

"Somboon!" the weathered man shouted over his shoulder. A thin man in a stained apron came out of a back room. He pointed to Nick and Ben and the paper they held while speaking quickly in Thai. Somboon returned to the back and reappeared without his apron and with a knapsack on his back.

"He will take," the store owner said in strained English.

The guide looked at the tree drawing and spoke quickly, using a lot of hand gestures. They followed him from the store-bar and Nick handed him a stack of Thai Baht.

"More when we get there," he said, hoping the man would understand. Samboon showed no sign of whether he understood as he placed the money in his knapsack. He turned and walked away from them without a word. Nick and Ben watched, perplexed. Had they been robbed? Then Somboon turned and gestured for them to follow. They followed him around the back of the building and along a path with buildings on the right and thick forest to their left. Twenty minutes later, they stood at the foot of a path, the tree from Nick's drawing directly in front of them. Nick was grateful the journey was short. Somboon stood there expectantly and Nick drew another handful of Thai Baht from his bag, realizing that they'd passed this tree on their way into town unknowingly. Nick watched Somboon retreat.

"Ready for this?" Nick asked, turning to Ben. However, Ben wasn't looking at the tree or Nick. Ben's eyes were trained on the ground where a thick yellow snake had come out from the brush and moved toward Nick's foot. Before Nick could react, Ben scooped up the snake, holding it in two places along its scaly body.

"Hello, handsome," Ben said, bringing the snake to his eye level. Nick let out a breath he didn't realize he was holding and stepped back as the muscular snake wrapped around Ben's arm. Ben lifted the snake to a branch of the tree that marked the beginning of this portion of their journey. The snake uncoiled from his arm, and it soon disappeared into the branches.

***

Nick's skin began to itch as sweat ran down his back. They'd walked for hours in the humid forest air. It seemed to collect on their faces, making them both feel hot and sticky. They had walked in silence for the last few miles, the path winding in and around trees. The darkness of the damp forest became even greater as they walked further and further from the village. As the sun made its final descent behind the mountain, it became harder to see the path before them.

"Let's rest," Ben said. We can begin again in the morning. "What is it we are looking for?"

"On the side of the path, we'll find three boulders, each just smaller than the next. They mark the point where we'll veer off the path and continue traveling toward the cave. From the looks of the terrain, we may be in for a steep hike." Nick settled against a tree trunk, unclasping his cloak to remove his bag from off his shoulder. He removed a water bottle and drained the rest in two large gulps. Ben came up beside him and held out his hand.

"There's a water source just off the path this way," Ben pointed. "I'll refill our canteens." Nick strained to hear rushing water but came up empty.

"How do you know..." Nick asked. Ben just raised his eyebrows and gestured impatiently for Nick to give him the canteen. Nick handed it to him and closed his eyes as he listened to Ben's footsteps fade into the forest. Nick leaned his head back against the tree and listened to the sound of the forest. Birds chirped, bugs buzzed, and a light wind caused leaves to brush against each other. Occasionally, he'd hear an animal that he wasn't familiar with, perhaps a monkey of some kind. The forest had a whole feel of its own. It was its own being - breathing, heart beating, nerves spiking. Nick knew he was the visitor here. He heard Ben's footsteps return from the same direction he left and Nick opened his eyes when the footsteps stopped beside him. Ben held out Nick's water bottle, and he took it and eagerly drank. The ice-cold water was clean and smooth.

"I've never tasted water like this before."

"Incredible right? Living where I do, I had to learn to filter the water, so I wasn't taking in parasites or toxins. It took some trial and error, but it's second nature now. That water you're drinking is probably the purest you've ever had."

"I'm impressed."

"You think that's impressive? Watch this." Ben placed his hand on the trunk of the tree Nick was leaning against. Ben closed his eyes. Nick leapt to his feet and snatched his bag from the ground with a yelp. The tree he'd leaned on was moving. Ben had moved the tree closer to the one next to it. The ground rumbled as roots moved like waves across the ground. Nick looked up at the branches of the tree and saw them shifting, intertwining with the trees surrounding it. Within a minute, the giant leaves of the trees combined with the intertwined branches created a perfect shelter, the roof of the shelter just inches from the top of Nick's head.

"Wow, you've done this before," Nick stated as he placed his bag as a pillow against the ground, settling back and wrapping his cloak tightly around himself.

"Only a few times. I don't find myself in need of crude shelters in this modern world as often as I did when I was, say, traveling through Ireland during the potato blight trying to introduce different varieties of potatoes and helping farmers with their sheep reproduction rates," Ben explained, settling beside Nick.

"I remember that era, though we never worked together. I mostly worked with a Jewish synagogue in Britain. They set up ways to bring and distribute food among the starving. So much generosity during that time, but so much loss," Nick lamented. Ben hummed a sound of agreement. After a few minutes, he heard a rustling beside him and looked to see Ben sitting straight up from where he'd been resting.

"What is it?" Nick asked, alarmed, pushing up into a seated position. Ben held a hand out for him to be quiet. He stayed that way, listening, a look of concentration on his face.

"Ok, it should be fine." Ben said, laying back down. Nick felt too annoyed at Ben's vagueness to even respond. He lay back down and closed his eyes, ready to wait out the darkness.

CHAPTER 33

Nick watched as the light slowly reanimated the forest. Birds and other animals began their morning chatter. His ears became attuned to the buzz of insects. The air was dense with humidity and water dropped off the edges of the leaves above. Nick walked out of the shelter to find Ben leaning against a tree, deep in thought.

"I don't suppose it ever goes away," Ben said, throwing a handful of something in his mouth before brushing off his hands and turning to Nick. "The worry. Here we are, on a journey to possibly confront the Shadow itself, and all I can think about is if Allie sang to Rayne before putting her to bed."

"I think that means you're doing something right," Nick said, "but not having been a father myself, I can't say for sure." Ben snorted and shook his head.

"Are you not? The patriarch of the protectors, I mean." Nick stared, processing Ben's statement. His mind wandered to the Creator, telling him that the others would look to him to lead.

He'd definitely fallen into that role from the first day. "I think I preferred the brother reference." He shrugged.

"That may be more accurate, all of us being the same age and all. I'm glad Rayne will have uncles around. Unfortunately, I don't think you have any chance at the fun uncle role," he teased.

"I don't have any problem leaving that to Jack. I'll be the wise uncle she seeks out when her father is driving her crazy and she needs some words of advice."

"And just like that, I'm questioning ever introducing her to any of you." Ben tried to keep a serious face, but when he saw Nick's raised eyebrows and disbelieving expression, he couldn't hold back a laugh.

"I'll be back," Nick said, needing to find a place to relieve himself. He'd drunk a lot of Ben's remarkable filtered water. Nick wandered away from Ben, deeper into the forest. He walked back behind a large tree. Once finished, he walked around the other side of the tree and then froze when a rustling to his left caught his attention. He laughed under his breath at himself. It was probably a bird or rabbit. Then suddenly a blur of black fur rolled out from under a bush, landing on its back at Nick's feet. A cat sat up and looked up with black, glittering, curious eyes. Not a cat, a panther cub. Its sleek fur, shiny black nose, and bright eyes were enough to melt anyone. It took a step back and then pounced on Nick's boot lace.

"Woah, okay," Nick whispered, holding perfectly still as the cub tried to untangle its claw from his lace. He held still even when the claw poked through the side of his shoes and he felt a prick on the side of his foot. Nick hoped the cute cub would untangle and then run back to wherever it had come from. He watched as it became more entangled and realized he'd have to help. He slowly bent his knees down to a crouch. The cub let out an airy hiss, its little back arched. It tried to back away, but its paw was still stuck. The cub became more frantic as Nick touched its paw. It twisted and snarled and swiped at Nick's hands. He felt the sting of the claws across his left hand and saw the drops of blood, but continued calmly attempting to get the cat untangled. A loud rustling behind him made him and the cub pause. Suddenly, the cub doubled its frantic lashings, Nick's hand taking the brunt of it. He pulled his hand back and stood just in time to see a larger version of the cub spring out of the brush and launch itself at Nick. He wanted time to lunge for his staff, but knew he wouldn't be able to defend himself. He cringed against the incoming beast, closing his eyes instinctively. Just as he braced for impact, a yell and thud echoed louder than the roar of the attacking panther. Nick opened his eyes and came slowly to a standing position. Ben stood between Nick and the panther, his staff held out toward the giant cat. They circled one another and the panther snarled. Nick didn't dare make a sound.

"Nick, please untangle the cub," Ben requested firmly. Nick glanced at his left hand and saw the blood dripping onto the forest ground. "He won't scratch you. He just wants to get away from us." The cub trembled as Nick removed the laces from its claws and unwrapped its stuck paw. As soon as it was released, it immediately scrambled to the large panther. It sniffed at the cub and then looked back at Ben. It gave a harsh growl and then the panther and cub disappeared into the brush without a backward glance. Nick let out the breath he'd been holding and slumped to the ground. He grabbed his staff and tried to regain the feeling in his shaking limbs.

"What are you doing all the way out here?" Ben asked, his breathing still fast.

"I drank a lot of water. I needed to, you know... and then the cub came out of nowhere." Nick defended. Ben looked at Nick in disbelief.

"Stay closer next time you need a bathroom break!" Ben said, exasperated. Nick returned to his feet, brushing off his cloak.

"Do you need a bandage for that? I left all my tea tree oil with Allie, and this climate isn't great for aloe..."

"It's fine. It's already healing." Nick said looking at his hand, the bleeding had stopped and scabs were already forming. "Did you know there were panthers this close? Is that what your cryptic answer was about last night?" Ben looked down sheepishly.

"Well, I mean, yeah, but I thought the tiger was more likely to be a problem than the panthers. I didn't think you would go along playing with one of the panther cubs!"

Nick's frustration flared.

"I was not playing with it. The cat attacked my foot." Nick stopped when he saw the corner of Ben's mouth twitch. Nick pressed his mouth into a straight line. "What were you having for breakfast before a panther almost ate me?"

"It wasn't going to eat you. She was just protecting her cub. She didn't appreciate my interference, but you're welcome." Nick looked at the back of his hand, already beginning to heal, and realized the magnitude of the pain that the animal would have been able to inflict.

"Thank you," he said grudgingly. Ben slapped a hand on the back of his shoulder.

"Let's get you some berries and go find the cave," Ben said.

After washing their hands and faces in the stream, and refilling their water bottles, they collected their bags and continued along the overgrown forest path. The forest became lighter, and the humidity dissipated, though not entirely. Nick kept his eyes trained along the right side of the path, watching for the rocks that showed the turnoff point.

"This is it," Nick announced a few hours into their journey. The sun beat down directly overhead. As they walked in the direction of the mountain, they could hear the sounds of rushing water in the distance. As the sound grew louder, they took a turn and dropped down a steep slope, their feet sliding on the damp ground, until they found their footing at the base of a waterfall. Nick recognized it from the vision and was relieved to know they were still heading in the right direction. He let the drops of water coming from the waterfall cool his skin as he and Ben took a moment to eat and recharge. Ben filtered the water and refilled their canteens.

"What is our next landmark?" Ben asked loudly over the roar of the waterfall. "What should I be looking for?"

"No more landmarks. We walk to the base of that mountain." Nick pointed to the mountain in the distance. Tension settled between them as they realized they were approaching the point of no return. They were going to find the Shadow. It was easy to walk in silence through the forest. Nick looked for the clearest path and Ben followed. They ate as they walked and took very few breaks.

As they came closer to the cave, the purpose of their journey seemed to intensify. Their footsteps fell with more intention and they trudged on, the foliage underneath them soft with each step. Their cloaks would occasionally catch on the plants they were pressing through but they helped each other get free and continued on at a steady pace. Nick's breathing became heavier as the incline of the land intensified. He glanced behind him at Ben and saw that he was focused on his footing. Before long, the mountain loomed before them.

"Do we climb?" Ben asked, looking up as he caught his breath.

"We circle the base; the cave should be directly on the other side." The journey around the mountain took another hour. They kept their eyes sharp, looking up and around for any signs. They didn't see any until Nick felt a tug on the back of his cloak. He stopped and turned to Ben.

"Where are the animals?" Ben asked, looking around. "I haven't seen or heard any for the last quarter of an hour." Nick hadn't noticed, but was now very aware of the silence that surrounded them. The only sound was their breathing and the rustling of the trees in the afternoon breeze.

"Let's go." Nick picked up his pace and Ben followed suit. As they rounded the northern edge of the mountain, Nick's cloak billowed out behind him, caught in an icy blast of air. He looked up and saw clouds gathering in the sky, casting them into darkness. There was a charge in the air. This wasn't a regular storm. He could feel it deep inside. It carried a feeling of darkness and dread. He turned to Ben just as a bolt of lightning struck a tree ten yards away. The flash of light illuminated the area long enough to see his own panic reflected in Ben's eyes. Without a word, the two protectors broke into a run.

CHAPTER 34

Hands clasped tightly around the map torn from the forbidden book, Kaida stood facing the cave. The journey had been arduous, but the anger and hurt riling within her left her with no doubt about what needed to be done.

"Traitor... You've come at last." The voice was familiar from the council room a few weeks back. Despite seeking it out, it still caused a chill to run down her spine. She shook it off and approached the cave. Her eyes tried to focus but could not see through the darkness to the source of the voice. Two glowing eyes floated toward her as she heard the echoing sound of hoofs hitting stone. As it stepped into the glow of the setting sun, Kaida saw a boarhound. Its small size and unassuming nature would have caused Kaida to believe she was in the wrong place if it weren't for the animal's glowing red eyes. "You have realized the evil of this world and are ready to help me complete my work on this planet. Destruction." The mouth of the beast did not move as the voice echoed off the walls of the cave.

"I am here to release you. I will not help you."

"Why not my child? Together we could take down dynasties, monarchies, presidencies, all of it. Watch the glorious destruction. Once set in motion, we just have to stand back and watch as the humans destroy themselves." Kaida's mind reflected back to the dark alleyway of her nightmares. She had seen first-hand the evil that these people were capable of. Her heart turned cold at the thought and she met the beast's eyes.

"Destruction is your work, not mine. I am betraying my friends and will need to lie low. You do what you came to this earth to do. I will not stand in your way."

"Not even for Paul?" The shadow taunted. Anger and fear flared inside Kaida.

"How do you know…"

"The Creator is not the only one watching. I've seen your wounds. I see them now, in the shadows behind your eyes, the pain, the anguish, the loss. You wish to exact revenge. Strange how the one you revere as Creator would leave one of his own in such pain, such loneliness."

Kaida's hand shook in anger as she approached the invisible barrier at the entrance to the cave. How dare this monster speak his name? How dare he pretend to know of her pain? Paul was perfect, her everything, the complete opposite of the beast pacing the entryway of the cave just behind the barrier, watching her every move. She tapped the barrier with her staff and felt a shock run into the wood, a harsh vibration against her hand.

"I will not help you. I will watch and wait for the day of destruction, as the prophecy suggests, but you are on your own." Her voice held malice, betraying her great disdain for the Shadow.

"Understood, daughter. Release me." She hated hearing the beast again lay claim to her. She swung her staff above her head and plunged it into the barrier. The gold light from her staff radiated along the barrier with the sound of cackling electricity. The beast approached carefully and then crossed the line. A great laugh echoed in the woods around them and the beast fell on its side, squealing. Its legs jerked and then the unfortunate swine gave its final exhale. A dark shadow rose from the animal. It materialized into a ghostly dark form of a man. The only similarity between the beast and the Shadow were the glowing red eyes.

CHAPTER 35

Nick's legs burned as he continued his sprint through the trees. Rain pelted against his cloak, but he didn't slow his pace, a new sense of urgency filling him. Something was wrong. Nick recognized this path from the vision given to him in the council room. He knew they were close. The rain blocked the sound of Ben's footfalls behind him. Nick skid to a halt. They'd made it. The cave was exactly as he'd envisioned. Ben stopped next to him, leaning heavily on his staff. Their chests rose and fell in unison as their bodies tried to regulate oxygen intake.

"You are sure this is it?" Ben asked loudly over the pelting rain.

"Yes," Nick said, taking his staff out of its strap across his back. He walked to the entrance of the cave and reached forward with his staff. There was nothing. He stepped into the damp cave, wiping the rain from his face. Nick saw a heap on the ground and approached with caution. Ben followed. They both crouched down to get a closer look.

"A boar," Ben stated. "It's been dead for hours."

"We're too late," Nick said, looking down at the unfortunate creature and then over at Ben, who met his stern gaze. Heaviness hung in the air. Lightning flashed in the distance and they heard the same sinister laughter that had haunted their minds carried on the wind.

The Shadow was free.

Acknowlegements

My heartfelt appreciation goes to Brooke Jorgensen for being with me from the initial chaos of sticky notes scattered across the wall to the polished final draft.

I extend my gratitude to authors Britney M. Mills and Cindy Gunderson for their constant inspiration, unwavering support, and providing me with meaningful employment opportunities.

Thank you to my Alpha, Beta, and ARC readers – thank you for taking the time to provide your feedback!

Lastly, a special thanks to Brett, who has yet to dive into any of my literary works. Perhaps this will be the one to capture his interest.

Thank you,
Sheree

About the Author

Sheree Elaine has a passion for books, chocolate, and yoga. She is a city girl that married a farm boy, and together they've jumped in and out of small towns for over a decade. Armed with a degree in Communications, she navigates her busy life alongside her husband, four kids, and a big black dog named Ren.